Born in Christchurch, 1965, Tania Roxborogh spent the first 25 years of her life travelling around the country. As a result of her nomadic childhood, she experienced much of what it meant to grow up in New Zealand in the sixties, seventies and eighties from tobogganing on the slopes of Lakes Ellesmere, to scuba diving in the Bay of Islands, from working in North Canterbury shearing sheds, to painting houses and warehouses in Whangarei. Though her growing up years were fraught with difficulties, some self-inflicted, most not, she persisted with her love of language and literature and graduated from Massey University and Auckland College of Education.

Tania, an English teacher, married with two girls, still manages to combine her life's interests with writing a broad range of books. She also has her motorbike license, has passed Grade 4 piano as an adult, and loves watching television and movies: *The Shawshank Redemption* and Monty Python's *Life of Brian* are her favourites. Tania is the Head of the Languages Faculty at an Auckland High School where she teaches English, Social Science and how to get by in a crazy world.

Third Degree

TANIA ROXBOROGH

Longacre Press

Acknowledgements:

The saying goes that it takes a village to raise a child. The same must be said for the creation of a novel. First, I want to thank Tessa Duder. It was she who leaned over and whispered "That's a story to be written," after listening to me tell a class of senior girls about my burns. Second, Fleur Beale is to be thanked for the warm bed, lovely meals and the many readings and suggestions as I worked and reworked the story. Finally, Emma Neale, my editor. A gifted shaper of images. Thanks to her for polishing my precious gem.

This work was written with the assistance of a Creative New Zealand new work grant.

The quotation on page 7 comes from Janet Frame's *To the Is-land*
(Vintage, Random House NZ, 2001)

Published with the assistance of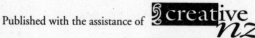

ISBN 1 877361 10 0

First published by Longacre Press, 2005
30 Moray Place, Dunedin, New Zealand

A catalogue for this book is available from the National Library of New Zealand.

Cover and book design by Christine Buess
Printed by McPherson's Printing Group, Australia

Contents

...time now became a whirlpool, and so the memories do not arrange themselves to be observed and written about, they whirl, propelled by a force beneath, with different memories rising to the surface at different times and thus denying the existence of a "pure" autobiography and confirming, for each moment, a separate story accumulating to a million stories, all different and with some memories forever staying beneath the surface...

Janet Frame
To the Is-Land

Our memories are card-indexes consulted, and then put back in disorder by authorities whom we do not control.

Cyril Connolly 1903–1974
The Unquiet Grave

Dedicated to my mother, Joy, for the ragwort summers, rainy autumns, gypsy winters and hope-filled springs. With love and admiration for these and a million childhood memories.

Eggs

"Oh shit!" I say, jerking my hand out of the microwave. Hot, splattered egg white and yolk cling, still cooking, to my fingers.

A dark-haired guy looks around from the sink. "You ok?"

"Burnt my fingers," I mutter, taking the pudding bowl out with a tea-towel. "Can't even poach an egg." I try to smile but I'm annoyed with myself.

"You should run that under water," he says, turning on the cold tap from the other sink. "Here!"

I dump the plate on the centre bench and go over to the running water. My hand has begun to hurt now. The cold stings and I want to cry but this is not the place. Instead I say, "Forgotten how sore a burn can be."

He looks up from his dishes. "Yeah, well, those microwaves are deadly."

To distract myself from the pain, I try conversation. "Dad said I'd either starve to death or kill myself with food poisoning. Don't think he thought cooking an egg could be fatal, even for me."

"Well if that doesn't build your self-confidence, I don't know what will." He pulls the plug and takes the tea-towel from his shoulder. "I'm Anton, by the way. Ph.D., second year."

"Hi," I nod. "I'm Ruth. B.A., first year." I rotate my hand under the water, still aware of the stinging, trying to look like

9

I'm not really hurting. "Ph.D., huh? How long have you lived here?"

"This is my fourth year. I went flatting once but it was too expensive. I get a bit of a discount 'cause I help out the hostel manager, you know, keeping an eye on things when he's away, making sure there's toilet paper in the loos."

He stands beside me, staring at my hand and that makes me shy so I try a joke. "This might be the only thing that gets cooked for my dinner," I grimace. "I could almost be tempted to say I miss Mum's cooking."

He laughs. It is deep and husky and very, very nice. "You homesick?"

I shake my head firmly. "Doubt it! I couldn't wait to come down here," I reply, thinking about how nice it is to be away from the rules, the routines that aren't mine. "Apart from doing dumb stuff like this," I say, holding up my hand, "it's cool being here." I begin to turn off the tap.

"You should do that for at least ten minutes," he says. "Otherwise it will keep cooking."

I want to tell him I know. But I don't want to draw attention to that. So instead I say, "Do most first years get homesick?"

"Hell yeah," he laughs. "For the first few weeks, no one can get on the phone 'cause everyone's ringing home." He gathers up his stuff but does not go yet. "You would think that by nineteen or twenty, people wouldn't need their mums any more, eh?"

"I'm used to it." I'm trying to impress just a little. "I've been getting used to doing things without my mum for nearly a decade."

He frowns. "Sorry. I didn't mean to be flippant."

I realise what he thinks. "Oh, no. Mum's still fit and healthy and bossing Dad around. It's just that …" But, I don't know how to explain it; how to put the way I feel about her into words and how and when and why things changed for us. Instead, I give the safe explanation. "She's bred me to be independent."

Now he smiles. "Nothing wrong with that. Sounds like she's done the right thing." He picks up his box of cooking gear. "My room's twenty-seven, down past the board room. If you ever need anything …" He blushes slightly.

"Like bog paper, you mean?" I tease.

"Exactly." He heads out of the cooking room. "See you around, Ruth."

I'm smiling when I turn off the tap. He's nice and he seemed to want to talk to me. I dry my hand carefully with the tea-towel. On the outside, my hand is freezing but by the time I've got out a pot to have another go at cooking an egg, the burning returns.

The dented saucepan breathes steam into the quiet kitchen, misting my face so that I have to wipe away the damp with my tea-towel. My fingers brush against an eyebrow, sending a re-minder of my outside self. As I wait for the water to boil, as I wait to place the egg into the bubbles, I wonder at how easily these fragments of childhood reappear to stand beside me as if they had just popped out of the room for a moment, returning now to nag, to chatter, to distract me from this day, this burn, this pot. This grey, metal pot with its scalding water.

Chapter One
Fire and Ice

When they ask me, I say I cannot remember. But, in my dreams, I am breathless with laughter running down the hall with someone chasing me. I will be caught soon. I am running into the lounge. I grab a hold of the kitchen door, the panelled door; cream, with scrubbed out paint on the edge. My fingers lock into the lip of one panel and I glance quickly back down the lit hall. The others are coming. I laugh, and using the door, and my fingers, I swing, I sweep around toward the kitchen.

I see grey and feel my cheek and top lip crush into grey. Hard, metal grey. I see stars and then the burning starts and my eyes are squeezed tight so the pain cannot get into them but the heat scratches my face, my hair. Rough hands pull me and I hear cries and calls and voices from under water and I am standing in the middle of the living room now.

A child is screaming and screaming somewhere but, when I look, the other children are silent. I hear the screaming but I can only make sounds in my head because it hurts so much. Mum is speaking to me but I don't hear her words. I only sense her fear and see her bravery as she takes my pants off, my socks off, my shirt off.

But, I call to her in my head, *but Mum, the boys will see me naked. They will see me.* Mum doesn't hear because she is mouthing sounds as she carries me to the bathroom and into the bath.

On the outside, the water is ice-cold but on the inside, it burns and burns and I want to get out. I try to get out but big rough, big sore hands are holding me down. Hot and cold. Heat and ice. Burning and freezing.

"Please let me out," the sound comes out of my mouth. "I would like to get out now," I say politely knowing that manners will always get me places. So, I am out. Shivering from the heat and the cold. Shivering. Shaking. Silently shivering and shaking as I am taken back to the kitchen.

I spy a grey metal pot and spilt water; its fire has already seeped away into the floor, leaving only a wet trail. Mum opens the oven door while Dad talks on the phone. "Come closer," she says.

"I can't," I croak, my lips wrestling with me, my cheeks stubbornly refusing to move. "I'm hot." But I am still shaking so they ignore me and pull me closer to the heat. The wave of oven-heat reaches out its scratchy hand and strokes me, rips me and I bleed clear drops onto the bare floor.

Mum is putting a sheet around me and I am pleased because the boys won't be able to gaze at me in the nuddy any more. Because they have been gazing, looking, their eyes wide: clear and wide. *Have a good jack?* I say in my head, through the heat wave. *Did ya have a good jack-nor-hee?* But, they don't hear my head-words.

I'm in the car, sitting in the front and it is so dark outside. Mum has her arm around me and Dad is driving, silent, his angry silence. "Mum," I say, "I am leaking." She switches on the light above us. I hold up my left arm and together we watch a bubble swell slowly while another has burst and is leaking clear water down my arm, soaking the sheet.

I am being carried up a lit path, my father still angry-silent, carried through a small door at the side. I know I am at the hospital because I have smelt this hospital smell before. The lady at the counter looks at me and jumps up. She rushes away. I have frightened her. I have scared her off with my bubbling arms and sodden sheet. Perhaps she knows I am naked too.

Someone else comes and then we sit and I pant sounds of pain, letting some of the heat out because everything stings so much. We are waiting and waiting. I hear whispers of other hurt children and beds moving for me.

Finally, *I* am put on a bed. A cold bed, the nurse says but she doesn't know that this bed is alive and it has prickly hot fingers too and I cry and cry. I am given a drink. The nurse says it will make me feel better and I am pushed through two-doors, and through two-doors again. I see Mum and Dad. They have masks on their faces just like the doctor and the nurses. Mum smiles and I smile but I know she cannot see it through my tears and my leaking face.

Now, it's just me, on the bed, looking up at the light hanging from the high ceiling. Lying on the bed by a window. The nurse is silent as she rocks back and forward, layering yellow mesh on me. On my arm, my leg, my chest. "Roll over love," she says as she pulls me toward her. I lie on my side, looking at the two-doors through the two-doors as she puts more yellow mesh on my back.

It is some time in the night; further night than when I came. I have escaped through the two-doors and the two-doors and I am going to go home. No one sees me walk down the corridor and past the breathing rooms. No one sees me push through more doors and I am standing in front of the lifts but I do not know what to do.

"Where are you going?" a white-clad body asks.

"Home," I cry. "I'm going home."

But, I am pulled into the ward and back through the two-doors and the two-doors and helped into bed.

I hear a nurse whisper, "What a mess," and the other, "She's delirious." I am given something to drink and I go back to sleep with a jacket of nettles around my shoulders.

Chapter Two
Strips of Skin

I know this room well. I have decorated the walls in my mind and I can see shapes in the peeling paint: horses and dogs and clouds and a funny man. I have watched unicorns dancing with snakes and seen them change.

Because I have to lie still, '*Lie still!*' all the time while the nurses pull strips of skin from my body. They use plastic tweezers with nasty ridges of teeth. One nurse has shown this to me and told me why they have to pick, and jab, and pull and tug at the bits of flesh that lie dead on my body.

There are three types of nurses. The first ones are the nice ones: they talk to me and are gentle and coo when it hurts and they always bring me ice-cream afterwards; the second ones are okay: they promise ice-cream if I lie still but never deliver. The third ones are the worse. They stab at me with their white plastic tweezers, pinching my skin when they miss and snarl when I cry or move or talk. They promise nothing.

They come every few hours and it takes forever. They even come in the night when they think I am asleep but I am never asleep. The room is always filled with the smell of the cream I am coated in. I will never forget this smell.

My oldest brother comes to visit me. I feel shy because I have no clothes on and no sheet to hide my nakedness. He smiles and chats about my cat sleeping on my pillow; about the hut in the haybarn; about telling them at school where I am. He chats but he does not look at me though I look at him. Look at him standing near the window, looking out; standing near the unicorn and the man in the funny hat. I wonder if I should point it out to him but I do not want to seem childish so I say nothing.

Like the others, he wears a mask.

My mother comes to visit me. She tells me about my cat sleeping on my pillow, about the new farmhand, about the cake she'd made for me and would have given me but the nurses took it from her. She holds my hand and asks me how I am. "Fine," I say. "I am fine." Then a nurse comes to pluck at my body again and Mum has to leave.

The nurse starts with my face, on my forehead. She lays a small cloth on my shoulder and, as she pulls off the skin, wipes it on the cloth. She smells of soap and has tight hair. Out of the corner of my eye, I watch the mask suck in and out with her breathing. In front of me, the unicorn's horn has pulled free from the wall and hangs in strips, just like my skin.

I want to tell the nurse to take her tweezers and do to the wall what she is doing to me but I am afraid of her. So, I say nothing.

Jab, jab, jab, wipe; jab, jab, jab, wipe. She tugs at me roughly and I wonder if she is unhappy, with her tight hair and her cruel fingers. Pinch, pull, tug, wipe. I stare at the clock and watch the hands jump in time to the nurse's work. It jumps for me because I cannot jump.

"Lie still," I am told though I have not moved. I need to go to the toilet but I have to use a bedpan as I am forbidden to go past the two-doors. Soon, I am busting and I have to tell her. I turn my head to speak just as she reaches up for another piece of skin.

The instrument stabs me in the cheek and the pain shoots through me and out the other side. I am crying now, but the nurse is muttering.

"I told you to lie still, you silly girl," she growls.

"I need to go to the toilet," I sob.

The nurse snorts, throws the tweezers into a bowl and pushes away from the bed.

She does not help me and I go over to the corner of the room and wee into the bedpan, feeling shy, feeling shamed. My cheek tickles and I dab it with the toilet paper. It comes back with blood on it. I look over at the nurse but she is staring out the window, tapping her fingers on the side cabinet.

I cover the pan as I have been shown and climb back on the bed. I am still without clothes and I wish I could just have a sheet to cover my lower half.

The treatment continues and I close my eyes.

I have been in here for a week now and the skin on my arm and leg has stopped dying. I can have a sheet and some hospital pyjamas but only the bottoms. Mum has not been back to see me so my day is divided into torture shifts. I am staring at the ceiling trying to make sense of the patterns of mould in the corner by the window. It swirls and blurs in front of my eyes. I am bored. There is nothing to do in this room with its two-doors, two-doors, where those who come hide behind white masks.

I sit up and study my arm. The burned flesh runs from under my arm by my armpit, over the top (opposite side to the elbow) and down the lower arm. The white cream is plastered and flecks of blackybrown skin mix in.

With my right-hand fingers, I rub the surface of the cream gently. There is no pain. I rub harder and touch the flesh underneath, wiping the cream aside. As soon as there is air, the pain stings me. I quickly move the cream back to cover the red, raw part on me.

A guy comes in. A guy dressed in white shirt and trousers and he is not wearing a mask.

"Going for a ride," he says cheerfully and swings my bed around so that my feet are facing the two-doors. We bump through and bump through again. I am free. No more two-doors and two-doors.

He wheels the bed a short way and swings into another room. There is already a bed in there. A bed with someone in it. A girl. A dark girl, with dark hair. With a burnt face. I now have a room-mate.

"What happened to you?" I ask, not rudely.

"Lit a match," she says. "Under a tractor. It blew up."

I nod. It makes sense and I lie back on my pillow. I look at the ceiling and the walls of this room. It has been freshly cleaned because I can smell it. There is no mould and no peeling paint.

I think, this is a good sign.

Chapter Three

Knock Three Times

There is less sun in this room but more laughter as Kiri tells me jokes, dirty ones, and we giggle at the rude words. Like the one about the man who used to put his thing through a hole in the wall and do it with a lady. The signal that she wanted it was to knock three times (just like the song my mum sings). One day a cleaner came to clean the lady's house and her broom banged against the wall, three times. Next thing, the man puts his thing through and the cleaning lady screams, *Eek, a bald-headed rat!* and whacks it hard with the broom.

We laugh and laugh at that one. I know it is funny though I do not really get why.

Kiri's face is pink and brown: the brown bits are flaking away because of the fire. I tell her she's not really Maori; that she is Pakeha under the skin. She says that her ma reckons it shows that we are all the same underneath. I wonder what is under my damaged layer but don't ask.

Two nurses come now and dress our bodies: Kiri's is over quick but I have to lie still, still while the patches of sticky yellow mesh are pulled free and new ones are placed over my angry red skin. Sometimes it hurts but I don't say anything. It is just a quick sting and I know that these nurses don't mean for it to happen. So, I hold my breath, thinking pain cannot live without air and I won't give it air to breathe so it will die soon.

It does.

It is never quiet. I can hear always the rattle of the tea trolley or beds or nurses' squeaky shoes. I wonder about how things are on the farm and if my cat is sad that I am not there to let her in under the covers.

I have not seen my dad yet and wonder if he is still angry at me. I wish he would come so I could tell him that I am sorry he missed his tennis game and that I made a mess on the floor in the kitchen. I wonder if the new farmhand has discovered my secret hut in the haybarn and, if he has, whether he will destroy it or leave it be. Maybe he will use it as his secret hideaway, too.

The matron comes into our room. I am reading one of Kiri's books and Kiri is reading a comic. The matron says "You're both going to the ward. Tidy up this mess. The orderly will take you to your new beds." And then she leaves, goes, with her thick legs and short sentences. I do not like her.

I close my book, *Call of the Wild*, and swing my legs out of bed. I am not sure what to do so I try to make the bed but my shoulders begin to sing with pain.

"Leave it," Kiri says. "That's the nurses' job." I am relieved that Kiri knows so much more about this than me. I think I will get back on the bed and read again but the bed is too high. Besides I am hurting now and it is too much effort so I sit on the large plastic chair and try to read but the words swim away from me so that even the story is distant.

"You want me to get someone?" Kiri asks. I am surprised because I didn't realise that I was crying again. She is brave because she has left this room twice and I haven't since I was moved here. She knows what is out there and is not afraid.

"I'm ok," I croak, thinking that, soon, the pain will seep away if I am still.

I have read two chapters to the sounds of squeaking and rattling but no one has come for us yet. Perhaps they have forgotten about us. I am cold and wish I was back in bed. Kiri is asleep and snoring and I am tired of the book.

I slip off my pyjama top so that I can move around the room without the cloth pulling against my skin. I try out the game I have been working on in my head. The floor has large black, red and white squares and I have to get from the doors to the bed by stepping in the pattern I have given myself: red, red, white, black, white, white, black, red, black, black, wh…

"Put your top back on," the matron hisses at me and I fall over, my heart thrashing inside my chest. I grab my top and try to put it about me but it is tangled and my back is hurting. The matron pulls it from me and dresses me roughly. "I told you to clean up this mess," she hisses again. She turns her head, "Guy! Take these children to room eight and then come back and clean this up before the Tooley boy arrives."

We are to be replaced, I think, as Guy helps me into a wheelchair. I have left Kiri's book behind and turn to say but Matron is shaking her awake and the door is closing behind me.

It is lighter in the corridor and noisier and Guy whistles as he pushes me. We turn sharply into a bright room and I screw up my eyes against the light. He parks me roughly beside another bed, a whiter one and easily lifts me up. He does not hurt me and I am pleased though shy because I have not done up the buttons on my top and my chest shows.

I push my legs under the blankets as Guy whizzes out, still whistling. The bed crackles under me but I am used to that sound now. Both curtains on my right and left are drawn so I do not know who is beside me. There is a bed opposite, wrinkled, lived in but empty and I wonder who it belongs to.

Above the door is another clock: it has a mouse face and smiles at me. I smile back but my cheek stings so I stop.

I can hear laughter coming toward me and then I see Kiri with her speckled face and her pink dressing gown. Guy is pushing her fast in the wheelchair and she is giggling. The tyres of the chair squeal as they turn into my room. She lands beside the next bed and I ease back onto the pillow. I am relieved that I have not lost my friend.

Chapter Four

Ward Rounds

There is a boy in the bed opposite me. He has shown me his leg. It has steel wire going into the skin and coming out the other side. He says it doesn't hurt but I don't believe him because last night I heard him crying.

I could not sleep because the noise of the corridor keeps me awake. And the way my back prickles reminds me of our hay-barn. I was remembering how we built the room in there, remembering where my brother shoved up bits of wood to stop the roof coming down because it could, and then it could kill you, so you had to be careful like not using candles for light, only torches.

In my straw room, I pinned up my drawings and put an old blanket on the floor so that the prickly bits of hay don't poke me. I had some paper and some pencils so that I could draw. I like my hut and there I did not mind the prickling feeling. I hope no one moves it.

A nurse bustles in and pulls all our curtains open so that we can see each other and see outside. She opens the top window a little and we can hear the roar of the world. I hear a truck beep, beep, beeping and wonder where it is going.

The nurse puffs up our pillows and pulls our sheets straight and tight over us and tidies away the things we have on our cupboards.

"You on housework duties?" the boy opposite me calls to her.

She continues her brisk work and, without faltering, answers, "The doctor is on his way. I want you all looking your best."

"Best you get some of us paper bags," Kiri says and we giggle 'cause it's kind of true that Kiri looks yuk with her splotchy pinkbrown face.

The nurse washes her hands in our basin and growls, "That's not funny." And she turns to stare. I look at the nurse looking at me. She smiles slightly and then disappears out the door and to the next room, her too-white sandshoes squeaking on the polished floor.

That boy is trying to pull out his blankets. "She'll get mad at you," I say in my small voice.

"They're too tight," he answers. He grunts and twists, rocking the bars and wires and pulleys that hang about his bed. Then, he stops and looks at me. "Give me a hand would ya?" he asks.

I gingerly slip out from the straight lines of my cotton sheet, careful not to spoil the crisp effect, and patter over to his bed. I smell something strange and then I see his leg and feel my tummy move sideways. "Yuk," I say, not wanting to stare at the cruel, black stitches, the crusty yellow which has formed around the wires, the wires that go straight through his leg.

"Yeah, yuk," the boy says. "Now, can you quit gawking and pull that end out?"

With my right hand (my left arm is too sore), I pull out the sheet and go along the bed undoing all that the nurse has done.

"My name's Jason," he says. "What's yours?"

Just then a flood of white bodies rush through the door and my heart leaps. The tidy nurse spots me, reaches for me, pulls me back to my bed. I can feel my blood banging in my ears and wonder why I am afraid. She puts her hand firmly on my bottom

25

to help me get up and I feel like crying because I suddenly feel homesick.

My vision blurs as she tucks me in and, though I try and try, I cannot stop the hot, salty tears which drip down my nose, sting my face and then land on my top.

"Hey," the nurse says softly, "what's the matter?"

I look up at her and try to stop: gulping, swallowing the lumps of sadness which have come up out of my chest. "I want to go home," I cry.

"There, there," she croons not looking at me. "You don't want the doctor to see you crying, do you?"

I shake my head but the tears keep coming. I want to tell her that she reminds me of my brother pushing me up onto one of the large horses and now I remember and want to be back there with its familiar smells and sounds, not here with its strange whiteness and fearful stink.

Now people surround my bed and the tidy nurse draws the curtains around us. The doctor has shiny blue eyes and a kind mouth.

"How old are you?" he asks, looking at me, right at me, smiling.

"I'm ten," I whisper.

"Ben?" he says. "What a funny name for a girl."

"No," I giggle, "I'm ten."

"You bend? Bend how?" He turns to the nurse. "What are you feeding these kids?"

I can feel my face stretch. "No," I call, "I'm ten. Ten."

"Oh, you bend Ben. Is he all right?"

Everyone is laughing and smiling and I am happy.

"You're silly," I say because I can be just a little bit cheeky with this man.

"I'm not Billy. My name is Doctor Murley." His gentle hands have lifted up my top and he has pushed me forward, looking at my back, looking then at my arm, not touching my neck. Still looking at me he says, but not to me, "Might have to graft here," then he gently tucks my hair behind my ears. "You're doing wonderfully. You'll be home in no time." And then he is gone, with the others, leaving only the tidy nurse to tidy up.

I breathe deeply and feel better than I have forever.

Human Biology

The hostel social committee has organised a free, end of term barbecue. I don't like sausages but I do like what else is on offer: beer, wine and ice-cream. Anton is serving the drinks and wears a stupid apron that says *I may not be perfect but parts of me are excellent* which is kinda corny but actually quite true.

Suzanne, who's in the room next door to me, grabs two plastic cups filled with wine and brings them over. "You fancy him?" she asks before she sits down, flicking her head in Anton's direction. I feel myself blush before I can even shake my head. "Thought so." She sips her drink. "Bit old for you, isn't he?"

I finally get a chance to reply. "No to both of your questions," I say, frowning but aware my voice has squeaked a bit just like it does when Dad's caught me out.

"*The lady doth protest too much, methinks.*" She's already finished and jumps up. "Want another?"

"I've hardly started on this one," I cry.

"Well, hurry up before you miss out." She stands over me.

"I can't just drink it."

"Yes you can. It's called skulling." She takes my wine and pours it into her mouth in one fluid movement. "See, just like that. Now, I'll get us some more."

I watch her head back to the drinks table but am bored with just sitting on the hostel steps. I've not been in this part of the grounds before, so before Suzanne gets back, I make my way down one of the paths so I can explore.

The sun hangs thickly in the west and it is still very warm. I wander down past old rose bushes and find myself in a secluded grove. But I am not alone.

Almost completely naked, entwined, a couple thrash together on a rug. They don't see me and I should turn away but my eyes are locked into the scene: his white bottom and thin thighs, her full breast, eyes closed, mouth open. Skin, pale, shining, smooth, beautiful. They don't see me and I should turn away but I can't help myself wanting to see and see and see.

Far behind me, a firecracker explodes. I creep back the way I have come, now embarrassed, now amazed, aware I've been tugging my neck again.

Suzanne is surrounded by a group of boys from the upstairs rooms and she is laughing. Everyone holds a plastic glass, drinking, so I go over to Anton to get one too.

"You go off for a run or something?" he asks as he hands me a wine.

"No, why?"

"Your face is all red."

I am mortified that I am so transparent – perhaps he can tell what I have seen; perhaps he can tell that I thought of him and me lying there on that blanket. Absurdly I think that he might just be able to read minds but say to cover myself, "Just been sitting in the sun."

He nods and I can't tell if he has guessed but I pull the strands of my hair down across my face just in case my blotches are screaming out my embarrassment as well. "Make sure you get something to eat," he suggests, flicking his head toward the barbecue. "This stuff can be tough on an empty stomach."

With the plastic cup at my lips, I murmur an agreement and obediently go to the sausages, though I would much rather stay and talk. Suzanne's high-pitched giggling follows me and I envy her ease with herself, with people, with boys. She is so lucky that she has nothing to hide.

Chapter Five
Visiting Hours

Kiri's family have come to see her again. Her brother hangs around the door. He doesn't like our room. I stare at him; he stares at me. I poke out my tongue and he goes to his mother, standing away from me. She laughs.

Jason has his curtains closed. I know why, Kiri knows why, but we don't talk about it. It happened the day before yesterday too. It makes me glad I am not Jason: not tied to a bed.

And, just like that other day: the smell. I stop breathing from my nose and breathe through my mouth. I lift the sheet to my face so that it cannot come my way. I say nothing but Kiri's brother says, "Pooh! What's that smell? Smells like something died!"

Kiri hisses at him. "Shut up, Sean. Shut your fat mouth you dickhead."

"Shissh, shissh," hisses Kiri's mother, "E hoha, taipa." I look at her mother waiting for her to growl, but she is pulling Sean past my bed and out into the corridor. She speaks to him, using the funny words like the old man who comes to shoe our horses. She speaks to him and then comes back in alone.

"He didn't know," she says loudly but they are all smiling and silently laughing because they want Jason to hear that Sean is sorry but not hear their laughter.

I don't smile because I am embarrassed and I am closer than

Kiri and it really does stink. I think, I won't stay. I will go looking for Sean.

There is no sun in the corridor. I look right to where the large doors are open and see people moving around, chatting and laughing by the lifts, those lifts that I tried to flee to. Then I look left and see Sean standing outside a room far down the ward. I walk silently that way hoping I won't be caught, hoping that the nurses have retreated while their kingdom is overtaken by people who are well.

I find him in the television room. I am surprised because it is quite crowded but I can tell those who belong because they wear the blue-striped pyjamas. There are four of them: a boy about the same age as my older brother, a little girl in a wheelchair, and a boy and a girl who each have plaster from their ankles to under their arms. They lie on their tummies, each on a trolley bed with large wheels kind of like a wheelchair.

Sean is sitting in front of the television. I want to sit next to him but I am too shy so I sit next to the boy/man. I smile at him and he wobbles his head toward me.

"Daaaa…" he says and I feel frightened. I don't want to sit here now but I don't want to be rude. He stinks, too, this boy/man, of wee and I see that his pants are damp.

"I'll get the nurse," I whisper.

He wobbles his head again. "Daaaaa…" This time dribble comes out of his mouth.

I move back out into the corridor and, keeping to the left so that I don't bump into anyone, I make my way to the nurses' room. There are three in there but not the grumpy old bag, thank goodness.

"Excuse me," I begin. They stop talking and turn to me.

"There's someone, a big boy, he's wet himself…"

One of the nurses sighs and stands up. "I'll get him." She puts her hand on my shoulder and immediately the pain lashes over me. I must have cried out because the nurse is apologising.

I shake my head. "Doesn't matter," I mumble, lying. "He's in the television room."

I try to keep up with her as she walks away but I cannot. When I get to the room, she is helping him through the door. "That's a boy, James, it isn't your fault. We'll just get you cleaned up," she prattles on, passing me.

The boy/man wobbles his head at me and says "Daaaaa…"

I feel bad. I don't know what's wrong with him. He walks like my Uncle Terry does after one of Dad's rugby parties, when Dad's getting him into the spare bed. I shiver, aware that though I am cold, my shoulder is still burning.

Now, I am unsure: do I go back into the television room or back to my bed? I peep through the door and see Sean has now joined the card game with the two in the wheel beds.

"Hey you!" the boy in the wheel bed calls. "Why don't ya come play too?"

They have all stopped playing and are looking at me.

"She's from my sister's room," Sean says and I am annoyed with him. He doesn't even know me. "She got burnt."

"Obviously," snorts the girl. She shuffles the cards. "You gonna play or not?" She asks me, not looking at me.

I come back into the room. The little girl is reading a book now though the television is still going.

"Okay," I say. "What are you playing?"

"Foo," the boy says. "Do you know it?" I shake my head. "It's like gin. Know that?" I nod. "Good, you'll pick it up as we go along."

The girl deals the cards. "Kings are foo," she says.

I look at the boy, who I like better than the girl. "That means kings can be anything."

We play. I listen to them talk: about the boy/man: "And apparently he was a great rugby player too. Played in the under-seventeens squad. Just goes to show eh?"

"Yeah, well, if it was me I'd rather they let me die." This was the girl. "Wouldn't wanna live like that."

I am curious. I want to know what they know. "What's wrong with him?"

"He hurt his head playing rugby. Got concussion too many times and then something went wrong in his head and now he's brain damaged."

Brain damaged. He didn't look damaged. Damaged. I roll the word around my mouth.

I listen to them talk: about themselves. They are twins. They've had an operation on their hips. I don't understand but don't ask. Sean does, though.

"How do you go to the bog?" he asks. The girl goes red and this makes me pleased for some reason.

The boy answers: "We have holes in just the right places." He laughs. "Means they can also give us shots in the bum, ain't that right, Sis?"

"It's your turn," she snaps back and I notice she is tucking her sheet under the stiff concrete of her cast, looking darkly at her brother.

Chapter Six

The Test

Today, there is a lot of noise. More noise than normal. And, more nurses. Nurses with trolleys and equipment and charts. They come into our room and clear aside all the curtains. We have just finished our breakfast and the trays have not yet been collected. I had cornflakes and cold toast with marmalade jam. The jam comes in little rectangular containers but is hard to open. I ate all my food today.

At home, we have porridge. Dad makes it after he comes in from feeding out. He cooks it in a large pot and it sets firm in our plates. We put brown sugar on it and then the cream from our cow. It is delicious. Dad makes it better than Mum. Mum's always has bits in it. It comes from the same packet so I don't understand why it is different.

Dad says the way you make porridge shows what sort of person you are.

The nurse goes to Jason first. I watch as she wipes his wrist with cotton and then takes a shiny silver thing. "What are you doing?" Jason asks.

"Just doing a test," the nurse replies.

Jason looks at me. I can see he is scared. "Will it hurt?" he asks.

"Not much."

She holds the thing like a gun over his wrist and pulls. There is a clicking sound and Jason sucks in his breath. His eyes are bright but he looks at me again and says, "Didn't hurt."

Next she goes to Kiri. "Why you doing this?" she asks.

"To see how healthy you all are."

"I'm healthy," Kiri replies, her nose going slightly up in the air.

The thing clicks and Kiri yelps. "Hey, that hurt," she says.

"Wimp," calls Jason but I notice he has been blowing his wrist.

"Shut yer face," Kiri calls back. "No brain, no pain."

Then, it is my turn.

"How does it work?" I ask, heart pounding.

The nurse turns the thing over. "It is like a dish brush but instead of bristles, there are needles. See each of these," she says pointing to the needles. "Each one of these has a little bug on it."

I look, trying to see them move. "No," she smiles, "bugs you can't see. Bacteria. We put these into your body to see how healthy you are: if you are healthy, then your body will be able to fight all the bugs no problem. If you're not so healthy, then you will get a little bit sick and then we can give you some medicine to make you better."

I look at the needles and wish I was back home.

"Give us your arm," she says quietly. "That's a girl. Now, keep still."

Click!

I feel like I have been stung and tears come but I will be brave.

"There, that wasn't so hard was it?" The nurse is packing up her things, writing something down and then breezes out of the room.

"The first person to get sick, owes the other two a Moro bar. Deal?" Kiri says climbing out of her blankets.

"Deal," says Jason.

"Deal," I say thinking, I have no money to buy anything. I wonder now, with the nurse doing this test, whether she will have time to peel my skin.

The doors bang and I jump but pushing through are the brother and sister from the television lounge, in their wheel beds. "Hello," calls the boy. "They poisoned you guys yet?" He grins.

"Move it," growls the sister. The brother pulls himself further into the room. His sister follows.

"We thought we'd come say hello. We figured if we kept moving they wouldn't catch us. My name's Tom. This is my sister Aleea."

"I'm Jason," says Jason. "What's wrong with you two?"

"Bung hips. They didn't catch it when we were little."

"Oh you guys," says Kiri. "My little brother told me about you."

Aleea is manoeuvring her wheel bed so that she is facing the other way. "Sean? You Kiri?" she asks.

"Yup. The tractor face case," she grins.

Tom is moving his bed backwards and forwards. "What happened to you?" he asks Jason.

"Car accident. This lady went right through a stop sign into our car. The police told Mum her kids were in the back fighting so she turns around to give them a whack then smash. We're history. I was in the back seat. My brother was in the front. He died."

"Sorry," says Tom.

"Yeah, Dad's still bad. He's in intensive care. I haven't seen him yet. Mum reckons I need to wait a week or so."

I stare at Jason. I wonder what he saw, with his brother and his dad. I think about my brothers and my dad and hope they will come and see me. I wonder if Dad is still mad at me and then a pain squeezes my chest. I wish I could go home.

Kiri is swinging her legs on the bed. "Let's go somewhere," she says.

"I'm a bit tied up," says Jason.

"We could push your bed," she says. "Come on. Let's go exploring."

"Are we allowed?" I ask, interested but nervous.

"Who cares? What can they do to us?"

"The matron's not on today," says Tom. "I reckon we should."

"Cool." Kiri hops off her bed. "Okay, Jason, let's unhook you and get going."

I grab a hospital dressing gown from my cupboard and climb out of bed. I open the doors wide and help Kiri push Jason's bed. I am excited.

Tom wheels back out the door and Aleea follows. We get Jason's bed clear of the door after three attempts, all of us giggling and then turn right towards the outer door, towards the lifts, towards freedom.

Chapter Seven
Lifts

In the haybarn, I am not afraid of small spaces. I am not afraid because I have had a part in making the hut. I know where each room is and how to get out. I know the secret places and how to get to them.

In the lift I don't like it. Tom and Aleea have gone on before us so it is Jason and Kiri and me. Tom said to go to the ground floor but I cannot understand the buttons. Kiri pushes one and down we go.

We stop with a bump and then the doors open. It is gloomy dark and there is no one about, not even Tom and Aleea.

"I think we should try again," I say, not wanting to go out of the brightly lit lift.

"Not yet," Kiri says pushing the button which locks the doors open. "Come on, let's have a quick look." I hesitate but Kiri is already behind Jason pushing. "Help me," she cries as the bed bumps into the side of the lift.

"Watch it," Jason yelps, the pulleys and levers and his leg rocking to and fro.

"Sorry." I take one side of the bed and help Kiri push it into the darkened ward.

Kiri goes back into the lift and pulls the door lock button and nips out again before the door closes on her. Without the light from the open lift, the ward is even darker. The only noise is our breathing.

"What is this place?" Jason asks.

"Let's find out." Kiri begins pushing the bed again toward some double doors.

"This is the same as our ward," I say, seeing the side room which is used as a waiting room on our floor, seeing the double doors.

"What does that word mean?" Kiri says, pointing to a sign above the doors. "Maw-guuu," she whispers. "Morg-ee-uu."

It dawns on me. "Morgue!" I say. "It is the morgue. We're in the morgue."

"What's a morgue?"

"Where they store all the dead people." I can remember how my mother and father had talked about the story in the newspaper where a lady woke up in the morgue just before the doctor was going to cut her open and clean out all her insides.

It is also the place where, according to my brothers, bad people take you to steal your heart and lungs. They take them while you're still alive and then leave your body in the morgue to be ground up into dog food.

"I want to go back," I whisper. "I don't think we should be down here," I add pointing to the sign that reads: **Strictly No Admittance. Authorized Personnel Only** in dark red letters. Dark red like blood.

"This is where they must have brought my brother," Jason says, staring at the doors. "I wonder if he's still in there."

Kiri and I say nothing.

Just then, the lifts rush open and we all jump.

"There you are." It's Aleea. "Tom's sent me to find you guys. How did you end up down here?"

"Dunno," Kiri shrugs.

"Well, you must have come down one floor too many." I notice she has not come all the way into the ward. "Come on. Press G1 not G2." She wheels herself back into the lift and the doors close.

We push Jason's bed back towards the lift. As we pass under an emergency light, I see that there are tears on his face but I don't say anything.

Finally, we manage to get the three of us back into the lift and I push G1. The lift bumps up and the doors swish open to reveal a bright, lively ward with floor to ceiling windows showing off the outside world.

It is strange looking at cars and lamp posts and trees and outside people from this height. It is almost as if I have forgotten what the world is like at ground level. But it is also strange because now I know what life (or death, more like it) is like below the ground. I shudder at the memory, thinking of whose bodies were through those doors and what might be done to them.

Tired now, and wishing I was back in my ward, I help Kiri again but I can tell that not one of us is very keen any more. In fact, Kiri's pinkbrown face has gone quite yellow.

"Over here you guys!" Tom calls, waving to us from a small sweet counter. There are other kids there too. A boy on crutches hobbles past Tom and then quick as a spark, whips the sheet from over him.

I stare. Tom is laughing and chasing the boy, his bare bottom pink against the white of his plaster. I am surprised because he is completely naked there and yet he does not seem to mind.

Finally he corners the boy, grabbing the prodding crutch he'd been using to fend off Tom. They are still laughing and then

Tom gets the sheet back and easily flicks it around himself.

"Little bugger," he says grinning. He looks at us again. "Come on."

We park Jason against one wall and go to sit on the chairs. People are staring as they go past which I think is rude. "Do you mind?" I ask Kiri nodding toward the people.

"Doesn't bother me," she says. "If people don't like my friends then that's their problem."

I am not sure why she says this but think it might be too rude to ask her again if she is embarrassed about her face.

There are no mirrors anywhere on the ward so she does not know what she looks like. I am used to it now and I have heard the doctor say that there will be no scarring; that she will be going home soon. Lucky her.

Aleea rolls past, her arm outstretched. "Here," she says. "For you two." It is two chocolate bars, big size. "And you," she says to Jason, chucking the block onto his bed.

"Thanks," we say together, pleased that something nice has come from this trip.

"Let's go back," Jason calls, his chocolate on his lap untouched.

We nod. None of us wants to stay here, on this floor, where the rules and rhythms are different to our ward; where too much is unfamiliar. I think the height is just wrong. So, we go back, leaving Tom and Aleea and the others we have not spoken to; back to what we know.

When we get back, nothing has changed.

"Do you think anyone noticed we'd gone?" Kiri says.

Her answer comes in the form of the matron who sails out of the nurses' office just as we come through the doors into the ward.

She strides over to us. "Where have you been?" she demands, her round face red, her eyebrows frowning. "I've been looking for you everywhere. Get back to your room now!" She sees the chocolate. "And, you can hand that over for a start." She grabs mine and then Kiri's. Jason has hidden his. "None of this sort of rubbish for the children in my ward," she snorts.

We continue pushing Jason, and I am sorry that I agreed to leave. Matron is very angry and is shouting at nurses who come scurrying toward us, fussing and growling.

We say nothing but climb back into our beds. I am so tired and my back is hurting. Even Kiri is quiet.

We are not there long before the skin nurse comes and, after closing my curtains, she begins the ritual of removing the remains of death from my body.

Seedlings

Anton has asked me up to the lab again tonight. I'll go once the library has closed. He found me here about 8 o'clock and had a read of some of the books I'd pulled off the shelves for my assignment. He doesn't pretend to understand them just as I don't pretend to be interested in his plants. I also don't tell him that sometimes the late night means I miss my 7 a.m. lecture.

But I really like him and I think he knows this. That's why he asks me to help.

The lights flicker at quarter to ten telling us to stop studying and go to bed, just like our mothers do, and like obedient children, those around me come alive, stretching, yawning, moving. I, too, pack away my notes, put the books back where they belong and make my way out of the building.

I love night time: the inky blue shadows and the fact that only what really counts is seen. Bright eyes, smiles, people's outlines. Sometimes, in the summer, at night, I even pull my hair into a ponytail. Not tonight though – it's freezing, so I hurry across the student concourse, past the H-block lecture theatres, to the ag/hort tower. The sky is dark and it feels like rain again.

There is a light coming from Anton's lab and, as I do every time, I put my fingers to my mouth and whistle. It is loud and piercing. I see him look out and disappear quickly. He will let me in soon so I stand outside the main doors.

People are impressed with my whistle. Though I am doing an arts degree, it is the one thing that lets me into the world of the ag students. I don't know of any other girl apart from Elizabeth and Mum who can whistle like that. Still, Dad thinks it's a bit of a waste of skill. He says: *No use if you've got shit on your hands or your arm up a cow's bum. How you gonna whistle yer dogs then, eh?*

He's right and Elizabeth and I have tried to learn to whistle without our fingers. The closest we can get is a *pewheet*! sound. Somehow it's not as effective.

Anton opens the door. "Evening." His deep voice sounds too loud here with the lino floors and quiet noticeboards. Perhaps he's not wanting to sound pleased to see me. I just grin and follow him up the three flights of stairs.

The lab smells funny but I don't tell him. There are shelves of jars in all different colours and shapes lining the walls and trays of containers on some of the benches. Anton's experiment is in a room between two labs. He shares this room with another Ph.D. student, but I've never seen her. She has fuzzy things stuck over the outside of her computer and her desk is always immaculate. Anton's isn't.

We do what we did last night: measuring the length of the seedlings and writing up the measurements. Then, he takes a dropper of some chemical (I've forgotten it each time he's told me and now I just remember it as the stuff that makes apples go ripe) and places an amount on half the seedlings. Already I can see a difference in their growth.

I watch him, keeping to his right side, my best side. Close but not too close. I watch his fingers, long, pale, clean, and notice tonight he has a rip in his shirt, his shoulder blade showing through the flap. I have an irresistible urge to put my hand on him so begin sweeping some of the soil from the bench to the edge instead.

We never talk much. Anton seems comfortable in silence and I am too. We finish at midnight and pack away his stuff. This is the part I like the best: walking back to the hostel. Tonight, we walk closely, our arms sometimes touching. Out past the buildings, it darkens: the road lights not strong enough to show us the way. Just as we get to the bridge, it begins to rain. I'm only wearing a hooded sweatshirt, which begins to suck up the wet drops.

"We'll get soaked if we try to make it back," I say. "Under the bridge."

"Watch your step." Anton takes my hand as he helps me, unnecessarily, down the bank. We get under the concrete and a moment later, the sky throws down its load. It roars and roars as if pissed that we escaped.

But I am still wet and shaking. "Here, you're cold," Anton says, unzipping his jacket. Instead of taking it off, however, he pulls me to him and wraps the edges around me.

My heart is thrashing and the shaking now has nothing to do with the cold. He smells so good: faded aftershave and his own body. I quietly drink it in, forcing my arms to my sides though I want to push myself into him.

"You smell good," he says, his mouth close to my ear. I turn my face toward his and we kiss, softly, tenderly, and I taste him and I am aware of a heat spreading from my lower parts and I push against him, my hands exploring his back, tingling with the touch of his skin. I feel dizzy and breathless, willing him to touch me too and then his hands are under my shirt, fingers stroking my back, moving up, under my bra…

"Stop," I say, breathless, suddenly anxious, stepping back.

"What's the matter?" he says, trying to pull me into him again.

"The rain's stopped." I tuck my shirt in. "We can go now." I can't see his face; don't want to see his face but I find his lips with mine and then kiss him. "Come on."

Obediently he follows me out from under the bridge and we walk hand in hand this time back to the hostel. My heart is beating too fast and I can't slow it down. It is not until we are in the main building that I feel in control. We walk to my room.

"You want to come in?" I ask, feeling brave again.

"Ok," he says, quiet, taking off his jacket.

I flick on the heater, take off my damp top and sit on the bed.

Anton looks uncomfortable so I switch on the bed lamp and switch off the main light. "Come, sit down."

He sits beside me and takes my hand. He doesn't look at me but gently strokes the inside of my wrist. I feel the burning in me again and move against him, my breast crushing into his shoulders as I kiss him on the cheek, my nose nudging his ear. He shudders and pushes me down on the bed, kissing me, his whole body lying down the length of me and the same headiness I felt under the bridge is there. His kisses travel over my face, down my neck and up again but as he goes to kiss my damaged side, I take his head gently and direct him further down where I have unclasped my bra, opened my shirt.

The roughness of his chin scrapes my breasts but I don't care.

He takes off his shirt and begins to remove mine but I stop him.

"Why?" he asks, his voice hoarse. But I don't tell him. Instead I allow him to get undressed and I take off my jeans and climb under the blankets. He sidles in beside me, shivering but holds me close again. "You are so beautiful," he whispers but I only giggle and kiss him, pressing my hips into him so that he is on me again and we are swept along with our touching.

Chapter Eight
Bath Time

This morning the nurse has told me that if I am very, very careful, they will let me have a bath. I have to keep my knee up and I am not allowed to wash my hair but I can sit in the bath. It is good news because I am sick of the stink of my body. The stink that comes out of my skin even through the layers of cream.

The water is pouring through a large tap when I enter the bathroom. The splashing sounds echo and, when the nurse talks to me, she sounds metal. I sneak a look at her to check that she is not metal.

"What are you grinning about?" she asks, not unkindly.

"You've got pretty skin," I say.

"Thank you," she says but her face reddens and she busies herself with laying towels on the floor.

I take off my top and roll it in a ball, embarrassed about the dirty marks on the inside. But, something else is worse. When I take off my bottoms, I see, in this dull light of the room, that I have grown some hair down below. I hope the nurse does not see. I don't think she does because she is now taking my hand and helping me into the bath.

I don't tell her but I am frightened. I know it is silly and I know I will be ok but I remember, I'm certain, the last time I had a bath: I was burning and Mum and Dad tried to kill the heat with the ice cold water but it didn't work and I burnt and burnt.

Still, she is telling me how to sit.

"Swing your leg over that rod, that one. That's right. You ok?" I nod. "Good, and that's it. When you want to get out, pull yourself up with these handles and, once you're standing, you can unhook the leg."

I wish I could lie down. I wish I could go under the water and clean away the scum and smell of my burnt flesh. But, not yet.

"Can I get this arm wet?" I ask, showing her my arm.

"Not this time. Maybe later in the week."

I nod, gently dragging the flannel up and down my right leg.

"I'll give you a few minutes by yourself and then come help you out," she says, getting up.

When she is gone, I look around. The room seems full of stainless steel. I know it is called this because we have just put a new kitchen bench in and Mum is pleased it is stainless steel. You can put anything on it and nothing will damage it. Even pots. Even hot pots with water. Hot water.

I rub the steam from the wall and can see the shadow of me. There are no mirrors here but I am still the same shape so that is ok.

The door sucks open. "Right now, let's get you out."

The nurse and her strong hands are helping me to pull myself up and now I am standing in the water. She dries me quickly so that nothing gets to my knee.

Then I am out and she is putting fresh pyjamas on me and even though it was only half of me, I feel better, cleaner.

When I get back to my bed, there is a book face down on the pillow. I turn it over and read the title *Our Bodies*. My heart beats a little faster because I know now that the nurse did see. I stuff the book in my locker, pull back the covers of my bed and climb in.

I wish Mum would come. I wish Mum was here so she would notice, not a nurse, a stranger nurse. Mum would not give me a book. Mum would know what to say and I could ask her, but she has not come. She has not visited me in this room yet.

I move down the bed and pull the cover up and allow the tears to come.

In my mind I see Mum moving through the house: smoothly, quickly but not rushed, pulling up the blankets on our bed, stuffing our pyjamas under the pillows, opening curtains here, a window there, closing a wardrobe door.

In my mind, I follow her as the bundle of dirty washing grows in her arms: my undies, T-shirts and socks from the boys' rooms, Dad's pants, a grimy towel from the bathroom. In my mind, I stay out in the hall because I do not want to imagine that room yet. Then, it's through the dining room – curtains, windows, papers, cushions – still with the bundle, and sweeping into the kitchen.

I stop my imagining. My heart is beating hard and my hands are sweaty. It is morning at my 'remembering home' but the oven is on, with its door gaping open. I want it to shut: it should not be open. This is my remembering; I am in control but I cannot close that oven door. I see Mum pulling through the pile of washing on the floor, sorting it and I wonder why she cannot see that the oven door is open, cannot feel its warm breath.

Maybe, when she has finished, she will turn around and continue her tidying so that the oven will have its mouth shut.

I hear the click of the switch and the familiar sound of the large flat knob twisted around and then the gush of water as the machine begins to fill. Mum straightens, sees me and smiles but is silent as she moves to the sink. I think, why does she not see the oven? Its breath is warmer and has filled the room. I want to turn away but I do not want to leave my mother.

She is washing pots. One pot is large and, as she washes it, it grows. But she does not see this. I try to call out to her but no words come. The pot grows and now it is not grey but turning red, glowing, but Mum does not see. I cannot breathe. I cannot call. I cannot move. This pot, this red angry pot will hurt her and somehow I know that the breathing open-mouthed oven is connected.

With all my will, I call out: *Mum*, I croak. She does not hear me. I try again. *Mum*! This time louder but now the oven is hissing at me, drowning out my voice. I must warn her because she does not see.

Mum! I scream

And then I am grabbed. It is the oven monster and I fight off its hard hot hold. *Mum*, I call again. *Look out*!

I hear my name but I fight on. Someone calls me again and then I realise that I am not at the kitchen door but lying in a bed, looking up at the nurse who has said my name.

I stop struggling.

I am so hot and my pyjama top is soaked. I go to lift my head and sit up but the room wobbles so I lie down again. "What's happening?" I ask.

"You were having a bad dream. And," says the nurse as she pulls the curtains about me, "I think you have a fever." I close my eyes. When I open them she is gone and I wonder if I am still dreaming but then she is back with a thermometer. She puts it under my tongue and then removes my sodden top. She takes my pulse, frowns, writes something on my chart, takes the rod from my mouth, squints at it, frowns some more, writes some more and says, "You are sick. I'll get the doctor." She disappears again and I reach over to get a drink of water. My arm is bare and I catch sight of the place where they stamped me with the needles. It is red and swollen and I wonder why that is.

Chapter Nine

Eels

I have been sick all day. So has Kiri. Last night, she threw up for ages and ages. The room was really stinky. Jason asked the nurse if he could be in another room until she got better but the nurse said that most of the children were sick so he was better off staying where he was.

Because he's at boarding school nearby, my brother can visit me during his lunchtime. He looks strange in his school uniform. "How are you feeling?" he asks.

"I have a headache and my mouth tastes terrible," I say wanting to sleep but knowing that if I close my eyes, I feel like I am riding on a roundabout, going around really fast. So, I keep my eyes open so that I don't be sick. "I feel like when we all got sick after swimming in the river."

He nods. "Yeah, that was a cool day."

Not for me, I think, remembering.

Dad had given us all two blue plastic dinghies for Christmas and after lunch we carried them to the river. Us little kids had to have the life-jackets and Mum had said that we were to stay in the boats but when we got down to the river, my older brother and cousins wouldn't let us. We had to get into the water and swim alongside. I could swim but I still had to wear the life-jacket.

My cousin Kerry, he came from the city and hadn't swum in

our river before, so he was really scared but I looked after him. We swam for ages. The water was warm but not clear and I hated not knowing what my legs and feet might be touching.

We got to the water-hole: this was our favourite place to swim because we had tied a rope onto one of the large branches that reached out over the river and the water seemed fresher here. You could sit on the rocks around the edge and bake in the sun. We did that on this day, watching the older kids having a boat battle in the middle of the pool.

We had brought some leftover food from Christmas lunch and, while we ate it, a flock of geese flew in and settled on the water. I threw them some bread and they rushed for it, squabbling, until finally, a smaller bird pulled it off a bigger one and rose up out of the water and away. Some of them followed it but the rest went back to dipping their bills and flapping and stretching their skinny necks at each other.

I had my legs hanging over the rock into the water, staring at the birds when suddenly, plop! one of the geese disappeared under the surface. I watched, waiting for it to come back up. It didn't. Then, plop! again, another bird went under but not before it let out a dreadful squawk. Then, again, plop! Another bird was sucked down under the water.

"Look!" I said to my cousin Kim who was sunbathing further up on the rocks. "Look!" I called again. "The geese are going." And, even as I said this, another bird disappeared.

That's when I saw them. Eels, the biggest eels I had ever seen, one gliding past me, a smudge of white in its mouth. It came closer to the surface of the water, still chomping on the goose. It was huge.

"Monsters!" yelled Kerry. "Sea monsters!" He scrabbled out of the water and sat, panting, on the rocks. I'd already pulled my legs out of the water but as I stood up, I could see heaps of the eels, swarming around where the geese had been.

Two stupid birds were still floating there but not for long. One after the other, the eels pulled them down into the water.

The older kids had stopped their mucking around to watch. "Awesome," said my older brother, pointing to one of the bigger eels. They almost tipped the boats over trying to look into the water. They were laughing but I wasn't laughing. I was thinking about getting back home, about having to get back into that river.

Everyone was yelling and calling. Kerry came to stand beside me. He was silent like me. Scared, like me.

"How are we gonna get back?" he whispered.

"Maybe they'll let us in the boats," I said, hopeful, but knowing my brothers and his brothers, this wasn't going to happen. I looked up at the cliffs trying to find another way of getting back, but there was nowhere to climb. The only way back was the way we had come – in the water.

Kerry turned to his sister. "Kim, tell them to let us ride in the boats."

"Guys, let the kids ride in the boats," she said. "They're pretty tired."

"No way," my brother called back. "They'll be ok. They've got their life-jackets. Besides," he said, pulling alongside the rocks, "there's not enough room for all of us and those life-jackets are too small for us. They can swim."

Kerry began to cry. I wanted to but I didn't want to let them know how scared I was. "Come on," I said to Kerry. "Let's get in further up." We picked our way around the rocks, both of us keeping our eyes on the water, making sure that no eels were going to come up and bite us.

Because they do bite. Dad said that once he hurt his ankle out fencing and he went down to the river and soaked his foot and along came an eel and took a bite out of his sock. Dad said it was just as well that Mum bought the socks too big 'cause otherwise he'd have lost his toe. Whenever I see his sock with the big hole in the toe, I think about the eel that ate it.

Eventually, we had no choice but to get in the water. Kerry was grizzling and his brother kept telling him to shut up. We both held onto the rope loop at the end of the boat while the others rowed back up stream.

Sometimes slippery things passed over our legs and Kerry cried out that eels were getting him but I just wanted to think that it was river weeds.

Finally we got back to where we had gone into the water and Kerry and I ripped off our life-jackets and ran home before the others could make us carry the boats. By the time they came back, we'd had a bath, were in dry clothes and were sitting on the back steps in the sun.

My oldest brother was angry with us. "You little buggers didn't give us a hand to carry the boats," he hissed at us as he walked past into the house. Kerry just poked his tongue out and pressed closer to me.

The next day, we were all sick. Every single one of us. Mum and Dad and Auntie and Uncle were running around the house with bowls and towels and flat lemonade. Mum reckoned it must have been something in the river water; Dad reckoned it was food poisoning.

We stopped throwing up by the evening but all of us stayed around the house the next day feeling yuk and weak. We didn't swim in the river again. I was secretly pleased because I didn't want to meet any more eels.

Here, now, in this ward I dare to say other things to my brother. "I didn't have fun. You were mean to us." I am feeling sad and want him to feel a bit sad too.

"Was I?" He shrugs. "I don't remember that. Just Mum and Dad fighting 'cause there was a hole in one of the boats." He pulls on his blazer. "I better go back. I'll try to come another time. Hope you get well soon."

I hear his shoes squeak down the corridor and I try to imagine him waiting at the lift, getting in, waiting, getting out and then walking down the street. I try to imagine him so I don't think about how sick I feel. I think about what my brother remembered about Mum and Dad and the boat and try to remember that too, but all I can think of is us being sick in our plastic bowls.

I haven't thrown up now, here in the hospital, but I wish I could. I know I would feel better if I could get rid of the horrible, painful feeling in my tummy. The nurses are not chatty today; they are grim-faced and flushed red and rushing between rooms. Our nurse spends more time with Kiri because she keeps messing her bed.

My head is pounding and I feel so hot. I can hear my heart beating fast and wonder how come I can get sick in a hospital. My burns are hurting again and I am tired. But, eventually, my nurse comes to look after me. She takes my pulse, gentle, with cool fingers, takes my temperature, writes things down.

"Can you call my mum?" I ask, close to crying.

"We have, sweetie," she says. "She can't come just now. She said to tell you that she loves you and everyone misses you."

I feel tears leak from the sides of my eyes and a pain press in my throat. "But, can't she just come for a short time?" I ask, trying really, really hard not to cry aloud.

"I'll give her another call when I've got a spare minute, ok?" she says.

I nod, knowing somehow that there won't be a spare minute for a very long time.

"The doctor will be here soon and he will give you something to make you feel better," the nurse says.

Just then Kiri throws up again and the nurse rushes off leaving me waiting for the doctor to come to make me feel better. I wish it was my mother.

The Morning After

It is a tui that stirs me but I haven't really been asleep. I have relished these two hours, not wanting to miss a second of the feelings. But I need to go to the toilet, so carefully, quietly so that I don't wake Anton, I slip out of bed, wrap myself in my dressing gown and pad down the corridor to the girls' bathroom.

When I come back, he is awake. "You snore," he grins.

"You talk in your sleep," I reply.

He sits up. "Really? What do I say?"

"I can't make sense of it," I tease. "Scientific equations I guess."

He lies back against my pillow. "Coming back to bed?"

I shake my head. "Got a seven o'clock lecture." I pile my arms with clothes and toiletries. "Don't want to miss another one," I say as I head back to the bathroom.

In there, I look at myself in the mirror. Look at me the way he might look at me: my face, chin, cheeks, neck, shoulders, breasts, waist, hips, thighs. How he might have looked, and touched. A smile changes the reflection in the mirror and, if I twist my body at an angle, you can't see the scars at all.

I spot the evidence of our loving in the bin and embarrassed, shy, I pull lots and lots of toilet paper from the holder and pack it in over the wrapper and contents. I wonder what he will think when someone asks for more loo paper. This makes me smile again.

In the shower, I glide my hands over my body but, this time, it is like it is new to me; it is like I have an extra sense of how it feels. My fingers stroke the bones along my face, down over my jaw to my chin and neck and shoulder and, like a blind person, like one reading Braille, these fingers of mine read the story of my burning. Now slightly blurred, but mottled and twisted just the same.

When I step out of the shower and dry myself, another thought comes to me: one that has not to do with the past but with my future. It's time I saw a doctor.

Chapter Ten

Bitter Medicine

It's hard throwing up when you have to be wary of the burns. The nurse helps me to lean over the bowl and uses a damp flannel to wipe my mouth. She has to be careful because of the blisters around my lips. I'm throwing up not because of what Kiri's got but because the medicine is making me sick.

I started taking this medicine yesterday after the doctor came to see me. He was different to the other nice one: he looked at my wrist, took my pulse and temperature like the nurse, scribbled on the chart like the nurse, and muttered some instructions. Not long after this, I was brought a little paper cup filled with creamy liquid.

It tasted awful: all gritty and thick and bitter. It reminded me of ragwort. I know what ragwort tastes like because I have eaten some and it is just like this medicine.

At home, there is lots and lots of ragwort. When we first came onto the farm, Mum and I used to spend days and days digging it out. That was before I went to school.

I remember it always being summer and warm and bright. I would help Mum to carry the bag of salt and she would carry the large grubber over her shoulder. We started on the paddocks close to the house and went around and around, drawing closer to the middle until all the plants had been dealt to.

And, boy, were they dealt to: Mum would hack at the ground

with the rusty tool until the root was naked. Then, with the heel of her boot, she would squash the exposed organ into a bruised and battered pulp. Sometimes I would help by jumping on the mess after Mum. After this, she would grab a handful of salt from the bag and sprinkle it over the damaged roots.

At first, every morning, I would run out to the paddock to see if the plants had died, but they hadn't and didn't forever, until, one day, when I hadn't been looking, there appeared stalks upon stalks of brown withered plants. Mum's system had worked. She told me that all good things come to those who wait.

I think it was good that the ragwort was dead.

Dad reckoned it would have been quicker to use 245T but Mum had been told by Tommo, the old farrier, that the only way to get rid of the stuff was to do it how he showed her. Besides, Mum had said, it's better if we don't have that poison on the farm. It wasn't good for the family.

Dad said that that was ironic considering how she had tried to poison us. After that, she didn't say any more about it. But we kids giggled. We remembered.

One day, Mum came in from the farm, her arms full of green plants and flowers and a big smile on her face. I loved it when she looked like that. When she looked like that I knew that she was happy and that meant things would be happy for me.

"Can I help?" I remember asking, following her as she strode into the kitchen.

"Sure thing. Get me the large bowl," she said, dumping her armful into the sink.

The radio was playing her favourite song and she reached over to turn up the music. We sang together: me on a chair beside the bench, Mum cleaning the greenery under the cold water.

"What are you doing?" I had asked, unsure of these strange plants.

"Making a special salad," Mum said. "This is puha and this is dandelion."

"Dandelion!" I giggled. "You don't eat dandelions."

"They're very good for you apparently and I thought it might make for a nice change to have a salad from off our land…"

It didn't smell very good but I didn't want to spoil Mum's happiness, so I helped her wash all the puha and dandelion leaves, shake out the water, and rip them before chucking them into the large bowl.

Mum added sweet smelling tomatoes and some red onions and put it on the table. She made me get everyone in for lunch.

It tasted disgusting! Even with mayonnaise, it was disgusting. My tongue went all numb and I thought I would spew. Dad spat his mouthful onto his plate.

"What the heck have you put in this?"

"Puha, dandelion, onion and tomato," she answered tightly, but I could see that even she had not taken another bite.

Dad began to pick through the salad, his frown deepening. Then he snorted and shook his head. "Puha, you say?" Mum had nodded, looking unsure. "Where from?"

"In the paddock by the bridge. That's where Tommo said I'd find some."

Dad sat back in his chair and roared with laughter. "This isn't puha, you silly woman. It's ragwort!!"

Immediately, all of us spat out our food.

"Ragwort? It doesn't look like ragwort and I should know: I've pulled out enough of the damn things."

Still chuckling, Dad lifted up one of the offending leaves. "This is a baby plant. The puha is right by the creek."

Mum put her fork down. "Bugger," she swore and I was impressed because it was the first time I had heard my mother really swear before. And then she was laughing, too.

After that, I didn't go into the paddocks to help Mum because I didn't like being reminded of that horrible taste. The only time I touched ragwort again was when I took one of the plants to school for show and tell. I showed them the different parts of the plant and told them what Mum did to the plants but I didn't tell them about Mum almost poisoning us.

Now, I wish I was able to go out and touch one of those plants rather than lying here, feeling bad and having horrible medicine. Now, I would rather be back home trying to eat that horrible salad than being here, sick, sore and alone.

Chapter Eleven
Remedy

I think the medicine is working because I am feeling a bit better and the nurses are smiling. Even the doctors are pleased, for they keep visiting me and asking me how I feel and taking my pulse and my temperature and looking at my wrist. Kiri is better too but not Jason. They took him out, bed and all, when it was dark.

There is a gaping space where his bed used to be. I am staring at this when someone walks into the room.

"Hello, pumpkin." My heart jumps. It is my father.

"Dad," I say, pleased. I reach my arms out to him but he only grabs my hands.

"You been crook?" I nod, tears filling my eyes. "Ah, well," he says. "You'll be out of here soon enough." He sits on my bed, not looking at me but looking around me.

"I see hospital life hasn't improved your domestic skills," he grins a bit, glances at me, then away. I stare at him.

He seems exactly as I remember but different somehow. He smells mostly the same but his hair is longer. Under his shirt, I see a white cloth. A cloth I have seen every day since I came. I now recognise the smell on him. It is the same as the one on me.

"What happened to you?" I ask pointing to his chest. He touches his shirt and I see that his hand is also wrapped. "Have you had an accident?" I ask, wondering.

"Just a scratch," he says still looking around the room.

"Where's Mum?"

Dad's blue eyes lock into mine and I see that his pale face has reddened around the neck and cheeks. "She's not too good at the moment, love. She's been pretty tired so I said I would come see you today…" his voice trails off.

"But," I start, thinking about what he has just said. "But, no one's come to see me. Where have you been?" I cry, now a bit angry. Sort of angry at Mum but she's not here so Dad can carry it back to her. My eyes begin to sting and I shake my head. "Why haven't you come?" I clench my fists against my thighs, chest hurting. "I've been so sick," I sob and Dad tries to hold me but I am still sore, still raw and he doesn't know where it's ok to touch.

"Ruth," he whispers over the top of my head. I cry, full up with sadness, choked with feelings I cannot name. Clumsily, we find a way to hug and Dad shifts on the bed so that my back is resting on his front, the zip of his swannie pressing into my shoulder.

"I want to go home," I say, knowing I can't yet but hoping that he can change things.

"I want you…" He clears his throat. "*We* want you home too, love." He rubs the fabric flat on my good leg. "The chooks are starving; the dogs haven't been fed in days…"

"What?" I demand, squirming around to see but realise he is only kidding. "Oh," I add, strangely disappointed that a little bit of it isn't true so that somehow I would be missed.

"Hey, I forgot." He untangles himself from me and reaches for a large brown envelope he'd dropped at the end of my bed. "These are from school."

I dab my eyes with the sheet and sniff loudly. "What is it?"

67

"I dunno. Your mother asked me to bring them." His voice wavers a bit like when he has to put down one of the animals.

I look up at him, alerted. Something might be wrong. "What's the matter?" I demand. "Has something happened to Bonnie?"

Dad shakes his head and smiles. "Your cat is just fine. She misses you – like we all do."

My chest squeezes again but I take a deep breath and rip open the packet. It is full of letters from the children at school: Room One have drawn lots of pictures, some with people on fire, some with smiley faces. Mrs Ward must have told them what happened. They all have the same message:

Dear Ruth, Get Well Soon, Love Room One.

There are four of these.

The next group are from the Primer Twos and Threes. More burning pictures and more *Get Well Soon* but with *WE miss you.*

"It's because I play with them sometimes," I say to Dad. The Standard One and Twos have written a card together. There is a list of the things they have been doing at school.

But, it is the Standard Four letters I really want to read. My room; my class.

Dear Ruth, says Karen, *I hope you are not burnt too bad. I hope you are enjoying yourself in hospital. I have a new pet lamb.*

Dear Ruth, says Ryan. *Dad let me drive the tractor on Saturday. Get well soon.*

Dear Ruth, says Natalie. *I am sorry to hear that you have been sick. I hope you don't hurt much. When you come out of hospital, we can be friends.*

Natalie is a big! fat! ugly! cow! She is mean to me. When I first came to that school she pulled my hair and pushed me into the boys' toilets. She told the other children not to play with me. She told them I had nits when I have never had nits.

I don't like Natalie but I am very pleased that Mr Fisher has made her write a nice letter to me. It is on her best paper. Good, I think. Good job. That will show that stuck-up, fat-faced, cow turd.

"You ok?" Dad asks.

I fold the letters away. "Tell them thanks," I say putting the envelope into my top drawer. "I'm tired," I sigh, leaning back onto my pillow.

Dad stands beside my bed now, jiggling his left hand. He does this during the ads. He hates the ads. He coughs a bit. "Well, I best be getting back."

"Dad?"

"Uh huh."

"Why are you hurt?"

"I'm not hur…" He stops and looks at his hand. "Oh, this. Well, I got burnt too, honey." He comes closer. "Not like you. Just my hand a bit and a bit on my chest. Still, they made me stay in."

"You've stayed?" This is not making sense to me. "Where did you stay?"

"Ward Three. Two floors down." He half sits on the bed again. "It was only one night. The doctor, he was too busy. He couldn't see me until the next day and they wanted him to give me the ok."

"Are they bad?" I ask, a bit afraid; wanting to look at them to see if they are the same as mine, but not wanting to look too; not wanting to see that Dad could get damaged.

"They'll be all right." He goes to pat my shoulder but stops just in time and lifts his hand to my head.

"I'm sorry, Daddy," I cry. "I didn't mean to … I didn't mean to run but they were chasing me…" I feel the tears fall heavily on my top and I need to blow my nose but I'm too tired to reach up for the tissues.

"It's not your fault, you silly goose. It was an accident." He moves in front of me. "Listen to me, Ruthie. Listen." I swallow and take a deep breath but still the tears fall. He looks me right in the face, right at me. "It wasn't anybody's fault. These things happen. I'm ok and you're going to be ok. Got that?' I nod, sniffing and dabbing my nose on the sheet again. Dad brings me over the tissues.

He sits with me some more and I know that he needs to go but I don't think I can bear what it will feel like in this room with him out of it again. I wish I could blow my nose properly but I can't so I just dab and dab and dab.

Then, the nurse comes in. "Hello," she sings and she pulls the curtain around us and sets up her tray of things.

"Have a good sleep," Dad says to me, smiling.

"Say hi to everyone," I say, trying to smile but my eyes fill with hot tears again so I blink and blink them away because I don't want Dad to be sad. "Say hi to Mum," I add trying to be good and brave.

Dad's mouth forms a line and he frowns. "Will do, Ruthie. Bye bye."

And then he is gone and the tears are back and I do not want to be picked at today; I do not want this nurse who has chased my father away, this nurse who does not know that I am lonely and want to go home, to my family, my mother; I don't want this nurse to pull off parts of me and put them in the bin. If she does, then I might truly, really, unravel and fall completely to pieces.

Prescription

It's been raining full on for a week and I can't sleep. It's not the noise of the heavy showers on the tin roof of the hostel; it's the pain in my ear. I've tried a hot water bottle and pain killers but the *goush goush goush* rhythm of hot blood through my swollen ear drum keeps me awake.

"You should go to the doctor," Anton tells me. He even offers to pay but I don't want to go. I hate doctors.

"It'll get better," I say. "I always get them when I'm stressed."

"But, it's been sore for ages. I'll come with you, if that will help," he suggests. "That way, I can get another 'script for condoms." I feel my face redden because I guess what he might say next. "Or, you could ask about the pill."

"No," I tell him. "I don't want you to come with me; I don't want me to come with me."

"Ruth, you're being silly. Why suffer when they can give you something to make you better?"

His words sound strange not only because of the thick liquid behind my middle ear but because I have heard that sentence before and know it doesn't tell the whole truth.

In the end, finding yellow ooze on my pillow seals it for me. No more pounding pain but I know, now, I need medical intervention to prevent further damage. And, if I'm brave enough, I'll ask about the other thing too.

"You've got an infection," the doctor says, pulling off the top to the instrument he's put into my ear. "You ok about antibiotics?"

I nod, wanting to end this consultation quickly but knowing I have to ask for more than he's offering. "Can you give me a 'script for some painkillers, and –" I hesitate. "And the pill?"

I get a look. Here it comes, I think. "Are you sexually active?" he asks.

I can tell I am blushing. "Yes."

"What form of contraception are you currently using?"

Man, this is so hard. "Condoms," I say.

His pen scribbles on the pad. "You should make another appointment for a smear test." I must look horrified because he adds, "We do have a female doctor if you would prefer." I nod. "Ok then. Well, that's all done. If you're no better tomorrow, come back in. You should be fine though. This stuff will work quickly."

I squint to read what it says. "I don't think I've had that antibiotic before."

"You'll have to check with your family doctor. Or I can get them to send down your file," the doctor suggests. "Anything else?" He smiles, grandfather-like.

As if a pounding ear and rampant sex aren't enough. "I don't think so."

"You eating well?"

Well enough for a poor student I think, but I don't want to stay here longer than I have to. "Yep."

He reaches under the desk and pulls out a flyer printed especially for us: wise words about healthy eating, STDs, alcohol and drugs, meningitis and hepatitis and other 'itises'. "And do make sure you finish the entire antibiotic."

Dariomyson, 250 mg. 3 x daily with food.

"Who makes this drug?" I ask, a feeling of déjà-vu floating through me.

I can tell he thinks it's a dumb question – he has put on his patient face. He pulls out his manual and flicks through it. "Hmmm. Oh here it is: Kelton Pharmaceuticals. They're in Auckland. Been around for ages. The first version of this drug kick-started them really. That was years ago, about the time I started here – some time in the early seventies."

I read the name again: Dariomyson. And I remember. I have had it before. A long, long time ago.

At the pharmacy, I feel like crying. Maybe it's the ear; maybe it's the things I have to do for myself now I'm sleeping with Anton. And maybe I'm angry because I am remembering back then and I don't want to think about such things now. I haven't the energy.

At the bus stop I open my package and pull out the bottle of antibiotic. While I wait, I read the information on the label: *3 x daily with food. Keep taking this medicine.* I unscrew the lid and there is the smell I remember as a child. Those chemists may have changed the look and the taste but they couldn't change the smell.

The bus sweeps around the corner so I screw on the lid and stuff the drugs into my coat. As I pull out my bus ticket and step onto the bottom step, the showers turn to heavy rain.

Chapter Twelve
Raindrops

The rain is whipping against the windows, and even in this concrete shell, I can hear it roar. Aleea, now in our room, puts her
hands over her ears and screws up her face. It is loud and we
can't sleep but I don't want to. It reminds me of home.

Sometimes, it rains a lot. It's fun, after a long night of rain, to
wake to see where the silent caramel water goes. Because it does
go – up over the banks of the river; up over the paddocks with
the ragwort ghosts; almost up to the haybarn but never quite;
almost touching the bridge.

A life of its own, Dad says. And we must be careful though
not afraid. Every year we have been on the farm, there have
been floods. One year, it even tried to stop us getting out but
we still did.

We were driving back from Sunday school and came over
the rise before Hunter's Farm and there it was. Spread out over
the road: a warm, taffy-milk coloured river of water. Dad was
driving and he didn't turn around. Instead, he lined up behind
the two other cars which had parked further down the road,
just before the flood.

He got out. "You drive," he ordered.

My mother climbed from her seat into Dad's. "Will she make
it?" she asked, leaning out the window. We kids watched as the

other cars waded into the water, creeping forward, down, down, down.

"Wow," my brother said. "Look how high it is." And we did look because the water was washing over the boots of the cars but they kept on creeping. "I betcha they get stuck," he said, legs dangling inside, bum on the open window frame, arms hugging the roof.

"Look how high it is on Dad!" my sister cried. "Mum!"

"He's all right, love," she replied, but I saw her face white and hard like when she has a very bad headache.

We were silent then, watching the cars move through the muddy water and then, one by one, lift up out on the other side. The group on the far side of the flooded road cheered and Dad turned around, a big smile on his face. "Ok. In you come," he called.

"Get inside," Mum growled at my brother. "And wind up the windows. Get all the stuff off the bottom of the car," she said to us girls. As Mum moved the car into the water, following Dad, we quickly put all the bibles and pads and jumpers up behind the back seat.

Dad was waving us forward; Mum kept her eyes fixed on him. We all looked out at the wide, wide river.

Suddenly, the water began to come into the car. "Mum!" we cried.

"I know. It's ok." But I saw her knuckles were white as they gripped the steering wheel. The water was over Dad's knees and still we were going deeper. It poured in, under the door, dirty and smelling and wet. We lifted our feet off the floor.

"Give it some revs," we heard Dad call as the water climbed up his legs. The car roared in answer and I wondered if it would float or whether we would sink, float away, drown, to be found a week later against the fences like the weeds and tree branches.

Then we started to go up and the water stopped rushing in. Dad was moving faster and Mum was following him. We were coming out.

"This is so cool," my big brother said. "Can I open the window again, Mum?"

"No," she snapped. "Stay put."

My brother frowned but turned to look out the back window. "Wow," he said, breathlessly.

And we were on the other side, and the car was stopped. We opened the doors and the water poured out as it had poured in but more of it was in the back so we kids started scooping it out with our hands.

Dad came over to the car. "She's a good old beast, isn't she?" he said, patting the bonnet of the car.

Mum was out, leaning against the driver's door. "This is the highest it's been. Will we be stuck in?" she said, which is what I had been wondering.

"They reckon it's going down," he replied nodding towards the group of people. "I've invited those lot home for a cuppa. And," he added, slapping his legs, "a lend of some dry gear."

Now, as I lie here, I think about that road and wonder if it is flooded and, if it is, whether people will try to drive through like we did. I hope not, because it is so dark and they might not know the road like my dad and they might drown. I don't like to think about people drowning so I sit up and switch on my lamp.

"Turn that off," Aleea says, grumpily. "I can't get to sleep."

"Neither can I," adds Kiri. "But it's the rain, not Ruth's light." She turns over noisily. "I am so *sick* of being in bed. They expect us to sleep at night when we don't *do* anything during the day."

"You must be better," says Aleea, her grumpy voice gone. "When you're sick, you sleep a lot." She presses the button on her bed which makes it tilt up. "That's what's so hard for me and Tom – we're not sick but we're sure sick and tired of these bloody casts."

She's right and I'm glad I'm not her. I couldn't lie still, locked in concrete for all those weeks. And, she can't do anything – not even go to the toilet properly. Yesterday, just after she was moved into our room, she was busting and the nurses were busy. Aleea was pressing and pressing her buzzer.

Eventually, one of the mean nurses came, banged in the red buzzer knob, pulled the bedpan from beside the bed and just lifted Aleea up – one leg – tipped up like some lid on a glory box. And I saw.

I saw her privates. After that I don't feel bad toward Aleea; I feel shy when I look at her now.

Kiri has turned on her light and is making shadow puppets on the ceiling. I stretch my arms out, hands shaped like my father has shown me: my dog will pounce on her rabbit.

"Get lost," Kiri laughs and turns her rabbit into a solid blob and hits my shadow dog on the head. "Take that, and that, and that."

I unclench my hand and turn it into a claw. "Gotcha," I giggle. My sleeves fall down and I see my arms. I drop them and forget my shadow game and stare at the strange marking on my right wrist.

The rash has faded and it's still a bit itchy. When I asked the nurse about it, she said it was normal. She said that it will fade away completely and I will forget all about it. She said it was because the medicine was so good, like a magic potion. That the lab people had made it themselves, right here at the hospital. Right here in that dark ward with the blood red sign that reads: **Strictly No Admittance**.

Now, I pull the sleeve over my scars, not wanting to think that maybe there is still someone in the bottom of the hospital, stirring a big pot with the yukky medicine to give to all the children. Thinking that maybe it is not a white-coated doctor or nurse, but really a witch.

I wonder how come I'm different to the others: the ones who are normal and whose bodies do the right thing with the medicine. I feel like I did when Mrs Ward was telling the class about how the rotation of the sun and moon affects the seasons. Everyone else understood but I still don't understand how it all works. Like I somehow missed an important part of the story when I'd looked out the window for a moment.

Just like I don't understand now why, when they say the medicine is good stuff, it makes me feel so bad. Nor why I needed it when the nurse said I was healthy.

I roll onto my side so I can see my other arm better. The skin stopped dying a long time ago but now an alien growth clings to me, has become part of me. It is swollen red and mottled but doesn't hurt any more. I wonder when the growth will find some other body to attach itself to and leave my skin to go back to what it was like before. Before this place with its medicines and creams, before the peelings and the torture shifts, before the hot, hot pot with the burning hot water.

Before all things changed.

Chapter Thirteen

Swimming in our Skin

Me and Kiri are down at the pool. Aleea and Tom are there too: skinny, white, sitting up in wheelchairs. Their casts came off yesterday.

It is funny seeing them upright, so little in their dressing gowns. Tom is quiet for once. Kiri said that she thought he had cried when his cast came off but when she asked, Aleea snapped at her to mind her own business.

They lower their wheelchairs into the pool, one at a time, where two grown ups wait.

I'm here watching but I'm not allowed to swim because I might get an infection. I wish I was swimming instead of sitting here, feeling too hot. The pool room echoes with our voices but I don't want to talk. It's a large pool but not as big as the one we have at school.

That one is outside and is old and crumbling with concrete seats which go up for people to watch you swim. Its edges have been nibbled at by some unseen monster which comes out of the pool at night when it's hungry. I don't like our pool and I am afraid to sit on its seats. It has large thick sides and iron steps which rattle when you climb them.

Tom is trying to swim by himself but the man reaches out and tries to grab him back. He only gets his pants and they come off easily. We all laugh and Tom does too, and goes under so that the man pulls him out, coughing but grinning.

· "It's because he's lost so much weight," says the nurse who is looking after me and Kiri. "That's why they just slipped off."

"It's nicer swimming in the nuddy," Kiri says, looking at the water.

"We have to," I say. "At our school, we all swim in the nuddy." Both Kiri and the nurse look at me. I know I have shocked them. "My school is much, much smaller than the one we used to go to in town," I say, trying to explain. "It only has one building but it has two large classrooms. Mr Fisher, he's our principal, he's in one and Mrs Ward is in the other. I used to be in Mrs Ward's class but now all our family is in Mr Fisher's – all except Mark because he boards at the high school here in town this year."

Aleea is squealing because Tom has splashed her so we watch them for a while as they do their exercises. I don't mind waiting to explain. It gives me time to think. Think and remember.

The first thing I learnt about our school is that our family stands out: not because we are clever or good at singing or sports or have famous parents or are rich; it's because we're white. All the other children at our school are dark. Dad was worried at first but Mum said it would be good for us. I don't see it any more but the first time we had to go swimming, that was different.

On that day, none of us had known it was a swimming day so we had not brought our togs and towels.

"Excuse me, Mrs Ward," I had said. "I can't swim today because I didn't bring my togs."

Mrs Ward was pulling towels out of a large cupboard. "That's all right, dear," she said. "We have enough towels."

I didn't think she had heard me. "But, I don't have any togs."

She stopped for a moment and looked down at me, her face

frowning. "I don't suppose you have," was all she said and bustled off out of the classroom into the sunlight. As I was the only one left in the room, I thought I should follow.

Everyone, including my brothers and sister, were already at the pool. Most of the children were either standing naked in line to rinse their feet in the rinsing pool or were still taking their clothes off in the changing rooms.

"Come along, Ruth," Mrs Ward called. "Into the changing rooms, please."

But I had nothing to get changed into. I looked to my big brother for support, his white, white body standing out among the group of dark skins. "Hurry up, Ruth, we want to get going."

I couldn't believe it. Only a couple of girls had their togs on. Everyone else was naked, boys and girls, and no one seemed to mind. But I didn't want to; didn't want to swim without my togs with other people who were naked.

I told Mrs Ward I felt sick so I sat on the steps and watched everyone else having a wonderful time.

Mum was furious.

"What sort of barbarism is going on down at that school?" she shouted at my dad.

"I'm sure it was all innocent fun," Dad was saying, fiddling under the bonnet of our car. "You know these places. Things are run a little differently."

"A little differently," Mum screeched. "God, it's disgusting!"

We kids were sitting on the front veranda watching them, everyone's hair but mine still damp from the swim.

My sister punched me in the arm. "It's all your fault," she said. "You and your big mouth."

She was right. It was me who was bursting to tell Mum about

the swimming naked, mostly because it was so bizarre, but also because I was mad that I had missed out on a swim and I was the only one.

Mum and Dad were still arguing. "There's nothing disgusting about a child's naked body," growled Dad.

Mum's face went redder. "You're impossible," she stormed. "Can't you for once support me on something?"

"What the hell's that supposed to mean?" Dad was yelling now. That was when we knew to go inside because none of us liked it when Mum and Dad fought.

After that, I always remembered my togs.

Join the Dots

I twist my damp hair, rope-like, clip it on top of my head and see that the thick clump of marbled skin of my neck is angry red. I must have been rubbing it. My damaged side stands out loudly, exposed in this bright morning light. I know make-up will calm it yet I don't feel like plastering my face today: it's muggy. But I want to wear my hair up, so I will just have to cover the scars.

However, before I have had a chance to subdue it, Anton appears. "Ruth," he begins, making me jump. "How did you get those...?" He stops, as if trying to find another word, a nicer word to name this distortion.

"Scars?" I say, aware my voice has hardened, is clipped.

He has come back into my room fresh and pink from the shower and smelling nice. The mirror grabs our eyes and we are caught, locked together, staring.

I have been waiting for this question, but anxiously, putting my energies into shutting off a piece of myself, pretending that there is no part in my memory that should require me to have to worry about such things.

Even when his fingers stray longer on *that* side, even with his silence when I turn my head away so he kisses me on the *other* side, even though I know he can see and touch, I have said nothing to explain.

Now, he has asked.

"I got burnt," I answer him eventually, saying the words which are owned by my family; the words which form the story which tells of my burning. "My father was getting ready to play tennis and we had run out of hot water. He'd lost his shoe and said that he would buy a Crunchie bar for the first one to find it. I found it and my brothers chased after me. I ran down the hall and into the kitchen and 'smack' right into Dad who was carrying a huge pot of hot water for the bath."

"Hell," he says. "Just your neck and shoulder?" He stands behind me and combs his hair.

I shrug. This story holds no power, no ownership over me. I tell him, feeling the words coming from my throat, the passage to my heart completely sealed off. My hand sweeps over my face, neck and arm as is the custom if I tell the story. "All over my face, my neck, my back, my arm."

"You were lucky," he offers, not unkindly.

"I know," nodding. I continue the telling because I have not finished the story the way this story is to be told: "My mother stripped me off and put me straight in a bath of cold water. The doctors told her that was the best thing she did although perhaps she shouldn't have pulled off my clothes."

He has begun to get dressed, the muscles in his long legs twitching as he stands with one foot on the bed. "How old were you?" he asks as he dries his toes.

I want his questions to stop because the storytelling has come to an end. When he looks up, however, I realise I did not answer him. "Ten," I sigh, remembering ten. "Sometimes I don't even remember it's there," I say, just to make him feel better although it is a lie.

He pulls a T-shirt over his head, and the questions still come.

"How long were you in hospital?"

There is a crumbling in my throat and I begin to fear that my heart has let through its clenched fist some of the ache I have stored away. My fingers tremble as I rub cream over my face and neck. They continue to tremble as I squeeze out the concealing foundation.

"Ruth?" he asks quietly. "How lo…?"

I interrupt. "About four weeks. One week in intensive care." The crumbling continues and, like acid, pain is bubbling up and I remember. "It was awful," I say. "And my mother only came to see me twice – the second time to take home." The words are spat out, like bile.

"How come?"

"God, Anton, do you want me to get my medical files so that you have all the details?"

"I'm just curious, Ruth." He flicks me with the towel though I am in no mood for it so he drops it on the bed and comes to stand beside me at the mirror again. "I want to know everything about you." His gentleness almost undoes me.

I'm still grumpy but don't want to be impolite so give in. "I have no idea why my mother never came to visit me in hospital."

"You haven't asked her?"

"No. Don't know why." *Why haven't I?* I think. *Why didn't I ever ask?*

His arms go around me and he gently kisses my neck; my scar; the place where I am damaged. I feel myself stiffen and he senses it too, so pulls away.

"Why did you do that?" I ask. "Why do you do that?"

We watch each other in the mirror. "Because," he begins, holding me again, harder. "Because I want you to know that…"

he shrugs. "So you know that every part of you is lovely to me. This bit," he strokes my neck, "I want to kiss it. For the time when it hurt."

I nod. I understand. "Thanks. But don't. I don't like it and I don't like the scars – they're ugly."

He shakes his head. "They're battle scars. A record of where life has taken you."

Then I am angry because he doesn't understand what it's been like having these scars, having kids at school tease you and saying that you're a slag, thinking they're love bites or people staring, wondering, until I tell them.

"I hate them. I wish I didn't have them."

"They're not that bad."

"Yes, Anton, they are. Every time I look in the mirror, I see them. If I had the money I'd get them taken off."

"Might ACC pay for it?"

"Haven't asked," I say. "Because that would mean doctors and tests and then going into hospital – something I have spent a lot of time avoiding."

"Fair enough, Ruth. I understand."

But he doesn't really understand because he's perfect and I'm not. And, he's not paying attention to my anger. Instead, he asks, "Is your Mum nice?"

I don't answer straight away. I want to be fair and keep to the facts but there's this pressing, familiar sense in my chest and I don't quite know who owns it. In the end, I say, "She's always helpful, you know, sending food and money and stuff," knowing that it's true and I should be thankful. But feeling something else. "What about your mother?" I ask, wanting to change the subject. "Tell me about her."

Chapter Fourteen
Mother's Day

My mother stands at the door to my room. I am reading *Little Women* and have been crying because I didn't know about Beth. It is only when I put the book down to blow my nose that I see her.

"Mum," I cry, the book falling off my knees as I scramble out of my bed, tissues forgotten.

She comes in and stands close. I put my arms up for her to hug, but I see that, like Dad, she doesn't want to hurt me.

"I'm all right," I say and put my arms around her neck. She smells wonderful, familiar, just as she should. But she looks different: she's wearing make-up and her clothes are saggy.

She lets me go and sits on the bed. "How's it going?" she says, smiling, taking my hand. "You need to cut your nails." She opens her handbag and pulls out her nail kit.

"Mum," I complain. "I don't want my nails done." I frown, thinking this is not what I want to be doing. "I'll do them myself later."

"Ok, but make sure you do. Ask one of the nurses if you need help," she says, putting her kit in the top drawer of my cabinet. "What's this?" her voice is strange and she has pulled out the book the nurse gave me. "Where did you get this?"

"One of the nurses," I reply, feeling my face go warm.

"What is she giving you this for?" She stops. "Have you had your period?"

"No, but, I …" I look to see if Kiri is listening but she's talking with her mum. "Down there," I point. "You know?" Mum is frowning, looking worried. "I've got hair down there," I whisper, feeling queer because this is my mother and I can tell her everything yet today things are not working out like I thought they would.

"Oh. Ok. Well, I guess that's to be expected. You are growing up and we'll have to get you a wee bra when you come out of hospital." The book goes back into the drawer. "Your sister got hers when she was nine; I was thirteen so it goes to figure you might get yours somewhere in between." She sniffs. "And I think I should go down to the hospital shop and get you some deodorant as well."

"How's Bonnie?" I ask, trying to get her off thinking about my body.

"Fat." We smile together. My cat is always hungry and would eat until she burst open like a big, fat tick, if we didn't hide the food.

"Last week, when I came home, she was sitting on the front doorstep with a huge rat. She was yowling away, as she does." Mum pushes her hair behind her ears. "I had to tell her what a clever thing she was to shut her up. I didn't want her waking up the kids."

I grin, thinking, imagining. "What else?"

"Ah, the farmhand seems to be working out. Does a few dumb things but your father says he's young and has to learn. Nan rang to see how you were and Poppa told me to tell you not to let the nurses give you a hard time."

Kiri's mum comes over. "Hello," she says, round face beaming.

"Good morning, Mrs Tito," Mum replies, smiling, and I wonder how she knows Kiri's Mum. "How's Kiri doing today?"

"Going home tomorrow, which is good. The dishes are stacking up, eh." She cackles as Kiri throws her pillow. It lands on my legs and I throw it back, poking out my tongue.

"Well, that's a relief for you then," my mother is stroking my hand. "It's hard going isn't it?" she says, almost in a whisper.

"And on them too," Mrs Tito jokes but goes back to kiss Kiri. "Taku aroha ki a koe, eh baby." She smiles at us and she trundles out waving. "E noho ra."

I go to say a joke to Kiri but she has turned over, her back facing us and I know she is crying again. Mum pulls the curtain between us. "I spoke to the doctor before. He says you can go home soon too, but he does want you here for one more week." I nod, thinking what will I do without Kiri? "But," she adds, now not looking at me but straightening my top blanket. "You will have to come back in for some skin grafts. Maybe not straight away, and only if you want to, to take away …" Her voices fades.

"Take away what?"

Mum presses her fingers one by one into the bed. "You've got some pretty bad marks on your face and neck." She looks at me now and is smiling her polite smile. "He thinks most will fade but some might not and you may want to have surgery on them … later … if you want."

"I'll be all right," I say, thinking that I don't want to come back here ever. There are tears in her eyes and that makes me frightened. "I don't mind, Mum, honest. Remember what Dad says? 'Evidence of combat' when you fuss over his hands? I'll be ok. I just want to go home."

"You are so brave, love," she says, still with that smile. "I'm glad you're feeling better because we were so worried about you." She stands. "I better get back. I'll catch you soon, ok?" She plants a kiss on the top of my head. "Hmm – and try to get one of those nurses to wash your hair – it smells terrible."

"Mum!"

"Well, as Nana says, cleanliness is next to godliness."

"Yeah and Dad says …"

She interrupts. "I'm well aware what your father says. I think I'll see about you doing some school work here too." She puts her handbag over her shoulder. "I'll see you later."

"Bye," I say, watching her leave, a heavy, sick feeling swelling inside me. I slide back down into the bed and pull the thin cotton blanket up to my shoulders. I'm trying to think what's wrong; why I feel like something is missing. It feels like at Christmas when you realise that there are no more presents to open and so a little bit of the joy disappears.

"You awake?" I call through the curtain to Kiri.

"Yeah," she sniffs but yanks the curtain back so we can see each other. "I hate it when Mum goes."

"You're lucky she visits," I say, feeling a bit mean. "What did she say to you to make you cry?" Hoping to make up for my meanness.

"Just told me that she loves me."

"Oh, well. That's nice," thinking that it's funny that Kiri cried because of that.

"But that's not why I was crying," she says defensively. "I had forgotten to tell her something and now it's too late."

I nod because I understand.

It's only when they bring us our hot Milos that I remember that I didn't ask my mother why she hasn't been coming to see me. I cradle the hot cup in my hands and sip the thick dark drink. It will be all right, though, because I can ask her tomorrow.

If she comes.

Chapter Fifteen
School

There are three of us: Kiri has gone home but there's Jason again, his leg in plaster, the wires removed, now in a wheelchair. Tom's here too, in his wheelchair. I have to walk because there is nothing wrong with my legs. I wonder where the other children are, though I know Aleea is down at the pool.

"Where's Kiri?" Jason asks.

"She went home yesterday," I say. "Why did they move you?" I ask because no one ever told us what happened to him. I thought he might have died but didn't want to say.

"I got worse," he says. "They took me back to the special room. I don't remember much except that I couldn't stop throwing up. That medicine made me worse."

"I didn't get sick," Tom beams.

I look at him surprised. "So, you didn't have to have the medicine?"

"Nup. Aleea did though. That's why she came into your room." I can see he's drawing a plane on his pad. "They still took lots of blood though. Man, I should have started charging them for the stuff. I'd have made a fortune." He grins at me. "You weren't too bad were you?"

I shrug. "Same as the others I guess." Then I remember. "Jason, how's your dad?"

It's his turn to shrug. "Ok. He's still in intensive care but he's

91

not going to die. Mum says his legs are completely smashed and they had to chop some bone out of his knee." He shuffles in his chair. "But, I haven't seen him yet. You're not allowed to visit if you're under twelve."

"In intensive care?"

"No, anywhere here. No kids allowed which is kinda funny seeing as this is a kids' ward. I haven't seen my little sister since before the crash."

"Lucky for you," Tom says. "I can't get away from mine."

My older brother is 13 but the rest are younger.

The teacher comes in and tells us her name but I don't hear it properly. It doesn't matter anyway, I think, because I'm not going to be here for much longer. I don't want to know her.

We're doing social studies about sheep farming in New Zealand.

"In the box," the teacher is saying, "are five cards. Each has a different type of wool on it." The box is passed between the three of us and we take one. "In your books, there is a description of different types of New Zealand sheep. I want you to read what it says and then see if you can match the wool on the card with the sheep in the book."

My hand strokes the wool and I feel my stomach clench in memory. The smell is just like the smell of my clothes during shearing time. I didn't think that smell could go anywhere else – that it just stayed in our shed. Even Hamilton's shed doesn't smell like ours.

Dad doesn't like sheep, but I do. He says they're dumb but he lets other farmers use our shed because it's a big one and quite modern: the shearer's stand is raised up like a stage and Mum reckons that's better for our backs.

I love shearing time.

It's always hot and we get up early, before the sun, and I love that moment when it's so quiet and muffled inside the shed as the shearers take off their jerseys and oil their combs. Then someone will go in and pull out the first sheep, tuck the front leg under their knee, pull the cord and *rrrrrr*. It begins. One by one, the cords are pulled and the combs buzz, hands flow, wool melts off, falling silently, fully, onto the board for the shed hand to scoop it up and throw onto the table.

My job was to pull off the matted dirty edges of the fleece and chuck them into the bag that held the dirty wool. I was quick and Mum said I was always such a good help.

At smoko, we kids would sip our tea from the large enamel cups and listen to the adults tell stories about numbers and rams and other farmers and things they did when they were kids. One day last season, a gang came to help shear a huge mob. They had two gun shearers so Dad said he would shed hand. They were so fast that he could only look after two shearers instead of three and Mum got me to sweep the board clear instead of work the table with her.

At morning tea, we sat around on the pressed bales and ate warm scones with jam and drank hot, dark tea.

"You kids like shearing time?" one of the shearers asked. His name was Jimbo and he had skinny, hairless arms and legs. He sweated rivers onto the board so that Dad was always wiping up the mess.

"Yeah," we said, pleased to be included.

"I like the press the best," said my brother Mark. "Dad lets me pack the wool down."

"You just be careful though," Jimbo said. "You heard about what happened to those twins up north?" We shook our heads. Everyone was listening now. "Well, they were hiding in the press but they fell asleep. No one knew and the hands kept putting the fleeces in and then the top went up and the weight came down." His arms showed the action of the press and I saw his muscles of his forearms move under the skin. "The bale was sewn up and off it went to town." He drained his cup and put it down.

"They searched and searched for those poor kids. It was only when a bloke in the woolstore opened up the bale for testing, did they find them – squashed flat as pancakes." He stood up and pulled off his jumper. "They had to toss the whole bale too." I thought I saw him wink at my dad but I wasn't ever sure. "Bit of a waste, don't ya think?"

Jimbo then sprang up onto the board, banged open the pen gate and pulled a sheep out into the light. The hum of the shears made everyone else jump up too. He could have been making it all up but I think I remember hearing about some children getting killed.

Still, after that, I kept away from the press and I saw that my brother worked the table instead.

I have finished my chart and think I've got all the wool matched right. We have a few drysdales on our farm and that's the one I know is right. The others I have worked out from the book. It has taken half an hour and I'm tired.

I put my hand up. "I've finished and I'm feeling tired. May I go back to my room now?"

The teacher smiles and comes over to my table. She reads my work, her red pen ticking off my list. All correct. "Well, done. Of course you may go."

I smile at her but when her back is turned I look over at Jason and poke out my tongue. He scowls but I don't care. This type of hospital school is pretty good if you can walk out after only half an hour, I think as I walk through the waiting area, through the double doors and back to my room.

It's only when I get there that I realise how silly I have been. School was boring but this room is worse: Kiri is gone and Aleea's still out. There is nothing to do and no one to talk to.

I wish I could go home.

Headlines and Phone Calls

I love Tuesdays this semester because I only have one lecture, in the morning, and it's New Zealand Lit. with Prof. Sandbrook. Then I have the rest of the day, mostly to myself, the large, old house emptied of its B.Sc. students with their three hour labs, the B.B.S. students with their Torture Tuesdays, the Dip Dairies doing their practicals. Just me and a few other B.A.s floating through the hostel.

I make myself a cup of tea and settle at a table. The morning's paper is still spread out from where someone has chewed over it, bits of jam sticking pages together. I tidy it up and begin again, turning the pages, pretending that it is fresh like it was this morning. Sipping and turning.

Minister won't resign. Sipping.

Air New Zealand chief quits. Sighing.

Police find man's body. Glancing at the clock. Anton will be finished in an hour.

Auckland on a knife edge. Like I care.

Children used in secret hospital experiment.

I stop. 1973. My date. The date of the year that was full of things I remember. I lean over the table and read. It is a story of tests, quiet tests taken, carried out, without the knowledge of parents. *For the good of the whole country's children,* the article quotes an old document. The details (hospital, city, test) are not exactly the same but it nudges something familiar. I stop pinching the marbled scar on my neck. Familiar enough.

Documents held in the National Archives show government officials decided parents of state wards would not have to be asked before a child was administered the experimental vaccine. This, halfway through the article.

National disgrace … Child abuse … Nanny State … These words leap out at me but are tied to the faceless people, important politicians, who are calling for an inquiry. Commissioner for Children. Church groups. Lobby groups. Everyone wanting to have their say.

But I think about the children.

I wonder who they were and whether they had the same sorts of things happen to them as us. I look at the inside of my wrist but can now only imagine where the needles went in. I used to check the site every week for years after but I don't remember when the marks finally faded. Other more important scars have taken up its place in my history.

The paper gapes at me and I feel nervous that someone else will see a parcelled memory. I feel anxious, unsettled. An emotion I am familiar with. So, I rip out the story and fold it, again and again, tightly until it can't be folded any more and tuck it into my wallet.

"Putting you through," says the woman and I am left standing, tapping my fingers on the wall as I endure pre-recorded phone music while outside some students are chucking a Frisbee.

"Records," says another voice, older, mustier.

"Ah yes," I begin, not sure what I am asking. "I was in your hospital in 1973 and I was wondering if I could get my medical records."

"Were you a maternity patient?"

"No."

"I'm sorry, then, all records pre-1980 have been removed."

"Why?

There is hesitation. "Ah, because we were clearing out some space." But, it's said with a lilting up at the end, like a question. Like, she doesn't know if that's true, or if that's what she's supposed to say. Like, there might be something to hide.

"Where to?" I ask abruptly, fearful that my bravery might slip away.

"I'm sorry, I can't help with that," the musty voice says.

"Can't or won't?"

"As I've said, I can't help you further." She wants to get rid of me.

Now what? "Thanks. Thanks anyway."

Bugger, I think, hanging up the phone. I stare at the article, trying to find a way in to that place that will provide sense to my memories. These memories which have swirled, unbidden, to the surface. My eyes focus on the by-line and I make another call.

"Putting you through now," says the receptionist and I wish that the group of guys who've come back early from the pub and are singing out of tune outside the door would quietly bugger off.

"Steve Shaw." A light, soft voice speaks.

I have to be quick; the singing has increased in volume and I don't want him to think my call is a prank. "I read your story. About the testing. On children." He says nothing, though I can hear the tap of a keyboard. I wonder if he's listening to me or is busy.

"Go on," he says.

"I was in hospital in 1973. For burns. I think they used me in those tests."

"You think?" a hint of sarcasm.

Someone knocks loudly on the door. "Come on!" a slurred voice shouts. "Let us in." There is laughter and then a chanting. "Let us in! Let us in!"

"Sorry about the noise. Someone wants to use the phone," I explain.

"I figure that," he says. "Go on."

The shouting is getting louder and I can barely hear the reporter. "Hang on a minute." I wrench open the door. "Piss off!" I snap.

"Wooooohh!" comes back their response, but I must have a look on my face because they get up from the base of the stairs and wander off down the hall, giggling, stupid. Drunk.

I go back into the phone booth and shut the door. "You still there?" I ask, now feeling like the moment is lost.

"Yes," he says but I can tell by the tone of his voice he isn't going to give me long.

"I know they tested me. And not just me. All of them. All of us in the ward."

The tapping noise has stopped. Steve Shaw is listening.

"Do you have any evidence? Papers? Documents?"

I shake my head though I know he can't see. "No evidence," I say. "Apart from scars. Scars and memories."

Chapter Sixteen
Routines

The doctor says I can go home tomorrow.

He says my scars are mostly healed and I don't have to wear the bandages on them any more. He says I can go outside but must not let my neck get wet, not just yet.

He doesn't say what I look like and he doesn't say that the marks will go away.

I wish he had.

I have stopped going to the school because it is boring and I would rather lie here and read: I have read *White Fang, Little Women, Jane Eyre, Oliver Twist,* and *Charlotte's Web.* I cried with all of them and Kiri said I was a sook.

But it doesn't matter now what Kiri says because Kiri is gone.

There's a new girl in our room. Her name is Casey, she's 12 and she has spina bifida but she doesn't look like the boy in the other room with spina bifida. Casey looks like me, normal, and can walk, although her foot is twisting in and she has to have an operation.

She's Samoan and her mum and dad are always here. Her operation was yesterday and she didn't cry at all. She's very quiet but I think she must be shy. Her mum is really friendly and gave me some cake.

Casey seems nice but I miss Kiri. When she arrived, I told her how things went in this place:

At 6:30 the night shift nurse comes in to take our temperature. She checks my dressing and then goes out.

"If you pretend you're asleep they won't talk to you," I say.

At 7:30 we get breakfast and at 8 the doctor comes to visit.

"Dr Murley's the nicest but he only comes sometimes."

At 10 o'clock, they bring round our drinks: hot Milo or juice for us and tea or coffee for the parents.

"I always have Milo. Sometimes there's a cake if a parent has brought one for the ward to say thank you to the nurses." I smile at Casey's mum.

At 11:30 lunch arrives. The lunch lady always wears a blue dress and puts our trays on the bed. Stainless steel again just like the bathroom. For lunch we get a piece of fruit (usually an apple or an orange), a drink of juice, hot fish pie (which is never hot) or shepherd's pie (with floury potato) or mince (with peas).

"Lunch is disgusting so if you can, buy stuff from the shop downstairs or get your mum to bring something in. But," I warn, "Don't let the matron catch you because she'll take it off you and they'll all eat it in the nurses' office."

At 12:30 they come to collect the trays.

"I always put the lids back on things because I don't want the lady in the blue dress to be upset that I don't like her food."

At 2 p.m. it is visiting hours. For everyone else but not for me. The tea trolley rattles down the corridor and people can have a cup of tea if they want. I stay in my bed for a while just in case but then go to the television room to see if anyone else is there without visitors.

At 3 p.m. the matron rings the bell and everyone has to leave. I hate this time because even though I don't have visitors, the ward is too empty when the outside people go. I don't tell this to Casey.

"We wait a long time for dinner," I inform her, warning her

in case she gets hungry like I do. "Five-thirty. It's usually the same as lunch but we get ice-cream and jelly or rice pudding and we get vegies like stringy green beans or soggy cauliflower or horrible peas."

"I don't like peas," Casey says quietly and I don't blame her.

"There's nowhere, really, to go – just the TV room," I offer. *Because you don't want to go anywhere else, curious. Who knows where you might end up: the sluice room, with its smells and strange marks on linen; the ground floor, where it's too bright and different; or, the below-hospital levels – morgue, basement – the dark places where people make stuff that might hurt you.*

I don't tell her about these things, thinking that she might be braver than me and go to see, making a trail like Hansel and Gretel so that, on her return, she brings back something bad from those places. Something else to keep me here longer.

"It does get a bit boring," I add, not wanting to make her feel bad.

Sometimes I sleep; sometimes I read. Sometimes the nurse comes to take my temperature and pulse but, since I stopped taking the medicine, that doesn't happen much now.

"Lights out at nine," I inform her, thinking of the matron and her twitchy nose.

Then there is the long night ahead and I don't sleep well.

My arm and back itch and sometimes I have to rub my shoulders backwards and forwards across the pillow to make it feel better. The nurses hate me doing this because it makes a mess but I don't care. I know they don't have to wash the cases or my tops.

Before, when I couldn't sleep, I used to make stories out of the patterns in the curtains but now I can't see them like I used to. Sometimes I sneak over to the window and read by the glow of the city lights though my eyes usually hurt after a while.

Casey sleeps very still, unlike Kiri who used to snort, and mumble, and sometimes thrash her legs.

I wonder if they will use the gun thing on Casey to see how healthy she is. And, I wonder if I should tell her to be careful of the chirpy nurses who come with their instruments and smiles, promising that it 'won't hurt a bit.'

I'm glad today was my last day; tonight my last night.

When I get home, I am going to hug my cat. I'm going to go to the haybarn and see if my hut is still there. I shall sleep in my own bed and not have to be woken up: by children who cry and cry; by nurses who talk loudly even though it's the middle of the night; by the sound of the lifts going up and down, opening and closing even though there is no one around.

When I get home, I will be good and not run through the house. I will be very careful and ladylike and not fight with my brothers and sister. I will do everything I am told to do and not make Dad mad at me.

And, I will remember to ask Mum why she didn't come visit me.

Chapter Seventeen

Homecoming

I sit on the sofa, my cat on my lap, watching my family move about as if I am invisible. My face feels stiff because I have been crying. It is all my mother's fault.

My mother drowned my cat's babies. Bonnie had given birth to four kittens but now there is only one.

"It's for the best," Mum had said. "We don't need five cats."

"But Mum," I had wailed, "She's *my* cat. You shouldn't have done that!"

I had gone to my room and cried and cried.

Now, I sit and watch.

I am wearing a bright orange skivvy with the collar covering most of my neck. Mum has put a blanket over my legs but I'm not cold; Bonnie keeps me warm. I am not allowed to go outside and I'm not allowed to play the usual games with the others. Mum says I can read or sleep.

I don't want to do either, so I wait on the sofa for people to come in and out of the house. The others are strange to me: my sister and younger brother have spots on their faces.

"We've had the chicken pox," my sister trills, grinning.

"I had eighty-five spots," says my brother. "Mum says because I picked some of them, I'm gonna have scars." He points to a crusty sore on his forehead.

"So?" I say. "I got burnt and I'm gonna have scars."

That shuts them up. They wander away and I am alone again with my cat.

My dad comes in for lunch. "How are you?" he asks, picking bits of hay from his jumper.

"Bored," I say.

Usually when I say this he answers: *Well, clean your room or go outside or help your mother or go feed the dogs or don't tell me you're bored.* Instead, he says nothing and goes into the kitchen.

"Mum," I call, still angry with her. "I'm hungry."

"There's nothing wrong with your legs," she calls back.

I try again. "I don't feel well."

She comes out and puts a damp hand against my forehead. "You seem all right."

I think of something else. "My tummy hurts," I say, because that is true.

"Well, come and get something to eat. You'll feel better." She disappears back into the kitchen and I feel the tears come again.

Bonnie stretches, yawns and jumps off my lap. I know she is going to find her kitten to feed her. She's a good mum. She's like the mums in our ward, the ones who came all the time and brought cakes. The warm spot where she was lying begins to cool so I get off the sofa and pad to the kitchen where Dad is sitting, eating and Mum is sitting, sipping her tea.

"What do you want to eat?" she asks not looking at me but giving my dad the look. The one that I hate because it means I won't be able to get my own way. The one that says they are getting along.

"A sandwich," I say quietly, sitting down at my seat.

Dad slurps some tea. "We'll have to buy in some hay. It's not going to get us through."

I look up. "The hay in the haybarn?"

"Where else?"

But – my hut. My haybarn hut with my special room.

Dad must know what I am thinking. He reaches over and pats my hand and I see the shiny pink marks of his fresh burn scar. "You can make another hut next year, Ruthie." I nod but the tears are there again. He pushes the rest of his sandwich into his mouth and stands up. "I'll send Cameron for lunch in a minute," he says and touches my mother's shoulder.

I look at them both. This is not what they do: touch and be nice. This is not my real mother and father and I look at them again, trying to find differences.

"May I be excused?" I ask, no longer hungry.

"Of course," my mothers says, not telling me off for leaving some of my food. I don't like this all being nice to each other because this is not what I remember so I go find Bonnie who is under Mark's bed with her kitten and pull them both out.

Carefully, I carry them back with me to the sofa and I arrange them against my lap while I wait some more.

Cameron comes in. I do not like him because he has a big nose and buck teeth. He always smells bad and my sister told me that he shoots the frogs down by the dam.

"Hello, Ruth," he says but I know that he is just trying to be polite.

I stare at him and his face goes a bit red then he goes into the kitchen. I can tell Mum doesn't like him much either because she has that tone she uses with people she doesn't like.

Dad comes back in without taking off his boots and stomps into the kitchen.

"Why'd ya tie the calf up like that?" he asks in his angry voice.

I don't hear what Cameron says but I do hear Dad. "Well, it's about time you cleared out those ears of yours and listened," he yells and storms back through the living room, out of the house, slamming the door.

It is quiet and I wait.

I hear Mum bang the back door as she takes a load of washing to the line. Then, Cameron comes out of the kitchen. He hesitates when he sees me and I poke my tongue at him.

Suddenly, he grabs me, his large hands twisting the collar of my skivvy and the pain slices through my neck. He has lifted me in the air.

"Shut yer face, you little shit," he snarls but I can't really hear him because I am screaming and screaming. In a moment he has thrown me back onto the couch and my foot knocks the kitten.

"Mum!" I scream. "Muuummmm!"

Cameron is gone, out of the house, and I can't get the burning to stop around my neck.

She is there, pulling my hands away, holding them with one hand while the other gingerly lifts my collar from my neck.

"It hurts," I cry. "Mum, it hurts."

"I know, I know," she is cooing and then Dad is there and the other children.

"What happened?" he's bellowing.

"Cam…ron," I stutter trying to stop the heat from having my air; trying to stop it hurting. Dad is gone.

"You kids, out," Mum orders and they disappear. Gently she takes off my top, careful not to touch the raw part of my neck. "Shit," she curses. "He's pulled off the skin." But I know because I can see blood on the neck of my top.

She wraps the blanket around my shoulders and puts me on the sofa. "Hang on a minute love." And then she is gone and I cry and cry because I had forgotten how much the pain hurts.

"Here," Mum is back with some cream and a bandage from the hospital. She gently wipes the cream all over my neck and the cold kills the burn and I can breathe again. "We need to get you to the doctor," she is saying as she is pushing me out the door, down the path and to the car.

In the distance I can hear Dad yelling and that makes me feel pleased.

An Explanation

I have told Anton what I remember. I have told him what I have found – the article in the paper – and about ringing the hospital and the journalist. But now I am stuck and do not know what to do with this information. Information which is incomplete.

I've also told Suzanne, who is helping on the student newspaper. Now, we three are counting Anton's plants again, during daylight, and drinking coffee.

"You could put an ad in the paper," Anton says, picking up a Gingernut and dunking it into his coffee. "Someone else might remember."

Suzanne snorts. "No one's going to own up to doing experiments on children."

I chew the inside of my bottom lip. "One of the other children may remember something but Steve said no one else has contacted him. And that was a news story."

"I could start writing letters to the minister or making a bit of fuss in the media," Suzanne suggests.

"Is that what you want, Ruth?" Anton puts his hand on my arm.

I shake my head at them both. "I can't remember enough."

Now it is silent again and Suzanne puts her cup down. "You know," she begins, "If you found out that something went wrong or some kid died, that would bring the bugs out of the woodwork."

I sigh. "It feels too hard, Suzanne. I don't think I've got the time or the nous to go finding stuff like that."

She frowns. "Well, I tell you what, if it was me or if I was a parent and I found out that something might have happened to one of my kids while they were in hospital, I'd be spewing." She stuffs the last of a biscuit into her mouth. "Bloody hospitals!" Bits of her food spit onto the bench. "God, they thought they were so right." I watch her grind an ant into the wooden surface.

When I look at her, I see my own deep anger reflected in her face but hers is caused by something outside of her, a reaction, a sense of injustice and a wanting to right that which was wrong. She's right to be angry with the authorities who allowed this to happen but I know that if my mother had been doing what she should have been doing, looking after me there in that ward, maybe this experience, this testing, wouldn't have happened to me.

Still, I don't want to get into that with them here. "Some parents had no idea, I guess," I say instead, thinking about Kiri and Jason and the other issues their families were dealing with at that time.

"You shouldn't let it go, Ruth," she replies.

Anton nods. "I'm with Suzanne on this one."

A current of anxiety shoots through me. I have spent so long hiding my scars, I don't know if I have the guts to bare them all. If I go further in this, I will have to draw attention to everything. But, if I don't, I will never complete the holes in my remembering and it's that which is worse for me.

It is after dinner, and we're in Anton's room for a change, lying together on his bed, quiet.

"What does your mum say about the testing?" he asks.

"I haven't told her."

"Why not?"

"I dunno. Don't think I can deal with the angst." I pull the duvet over my legs and tuck it around my back. "She's never been good with dramas anyway." Thinking about how she reacts when children hurt themselves, all clinical and business-like. "She's a bit of a cool fish."

Anton taps my hand lightly. "That's a bit mean coming from the devoted daughter."

I snort. "You're not talking about me, then."

He frowns as if processing what I've just said. "But you do love your mother, don't you?" he asks.

"Course I do."

He is quiet again but I can tell he hasn't finished with this conversation. Eventually he asks "Do you *feel* like you love her?"

This halts me. "No," I say truthfully. "I don't even think I like her very much."

"Why's that?"

I shrug. "I don't know. I don't remember ever liking her much."

"Even as a kid?" I can tell he doesn't believe me.

"Not since the hospital," I say, my voice fading. "Not since I came home from hospital." I close my eyes trying not to re-member but it is still there. "And then she sent me away to boarding school."

A horrible, painful time. I still recall the anger I felt toward her for leaving me there.

I used to walk past the main buildings and the girls from the top storey classrooms would lean out and yell at me: *Hey Ruth, who ya screwing*?

111

Usually, I'd head to the library to hide.

It was because of my neck; because they could see the marks. The doctor had told Mum they would fade in time and they had a bit by fifth form, especially after having the second lot of skin grafts in third form, but not enough. The doctor said I would need to get at least one more set of grafts done, but I didn't want to go back in again. I couldn't face the smell, the noise, the light – everything about hospital made my stomach ache with unease. It still does.

The school's librarian's name was Miss Larson; she used to feel sorry for me. She wasn't married but she was old and I often wondered how it felt to be old and alone. I wondered if I would ever get married with my mottled arm and twisted skin.

The girls, they thought the scars on my neck were love bites and I remember wishing they were but, at that time, I hadn't kissed a boy, never even had a boyfriend.

Dad always said not to worry about the girls: 'That's what it's like sometimes at boarding school.'

One weekend, when I had just arrived, the seniors made two of my friends pretend to be having babies and they were going to get another girl to kiss me but she didn't want to.

I hated the hostel.

That year, Mum came into town on a Friday afternoon so I didn't have to wait ages for the weekend bus home. I asked her if I could change schools but I knew what she would say: it's the only one with a boarding school.

I reckoned she could teach me at home. She said she had no patience and that I didn't listen to her anyway.

Like mother, like daughter.

Then, and now.

Chapter Eighteen
Cat's Claws

I am lying on my bed, on my side, with my neck wrapped in gauze, cream and bandages but I am not asleep.

My sister comes in and sits on the floor by my bed. "Dad's fired Cameron," she whispers. "You should have heard all the swear words." Her eyes are wide and I smile, pleased.

"The frogs will be safe, then," I say and we giggle.

"I'm glad you're back, Ruth," she says shyly, and I go to nod but then I remember my neck. "I looked after your Suzie." She gets up, takes my doll from her bed and brings it to me.

"You can have her," I say, feeling kind. "I have the kitten now."

"Thanks!" She looks pleased and disappears out the door.

I am alone again and I am crying, the tears dripping down my nose and wetting the pillow. I thought it would be better, being home, but it's not. I wonder if I might be missing my ward because, at least I would know everything that was going to happen each day. Mostly everything.

But, the thing that has made home bad, worse than the ward, is that I've seen what I look like.

I didn't think that what I could see on my arm and my leg would look the same on my face and chest: mottled, red, puffy. Over my cheeks and eye and mouth it is a little like when I got sunburnt but my jaw and neck look like my arm – as if some

113

sort of alien blob has grown there. A nasty, ugly blob.

The tears go on silently because I don't want anyone to come in.

Only, someone does: Bonnie. She jumps up on the bed and settles near my pillow. I can hear her purring and she sniffs my face. It tickles but I don't move and then she is licking me, like she licks her kitten; licking the place where the tears travel, and I close my eyes, relaxing. I can't have her in my hospital bed, I think, as her soft, breathy purr washes over me like the rhythmic sound of the ward. As I drift off to sleep I think, it's ok. It is ok to be home.

My aunt and uncle have come up for a visit. I don't want to play with Kerry outside – it's too cold and I don't want to get hurt. I also don't want to play with Kerry because I heard him tell Kim I smell funny.

Instead, I am back on the couch in the living room, reading with Bonnie on my legs. Mum and Aunty are having their 'catch up coffee' in the kitchen. I don't think Mum knows I'm here because I've heard her swear twice now and laugh at a dirty joke Aunty told.

"This came in the post yesterday," Mum says. "Dan's livid. He says he's going to go to the papers."

There is quiet. I guess my aunt is reading.

Suddenly, all the children run in the front door, past me, down the hall, down the hallway, outside again, their voices chasing after them. Bonnie, startled, has dug her claws into my leg. Angry, I push her off but I'm not really angry with her; I'm angry because I want to be like them and I can't. I rub the mad red mark she has drawn; rub away the thin line of blood which has streaked my leg.

A chair scrapes loudly in the kitchen and I sit very still, waiting.

It is my aunty who speaks again. "They did all of them?" she asks.

"I assume so."

"Why don't you ask Ruth?"

Ask me what? I wonder.

"Not yet. I'll wait a bit. Right now, I just want things back to normal."

I'm thirsty but I don't want to go into the kitchen because then they will stop talking and I want to hear what my mother will say. I want to hear if she will tell my aunty why she didn't come visit me much in hospital. Because no one's said. No one's remembered to explain this to me.

Nor why we all got sick.

Nor why a letter came that made Dad mad.

Nor why it has to be me, sitting here, inside, with these burns, while everyone else is running free and happy.

Chapter Nineteen

First Day of School

There are some new children in my classroom. They have come from Auckland and live in a cottage on the Davis farm. There are three of them: two boys who look the same and who are my age although I am two months older. The other is their sister — she is a year younger than me.

I don't like them. They are too loud and one of the boys was sitting in my desk when I arrived this morning. Mr Fisher said that I will have a new desk but I don't want a new desk. I have to sit by him today until they get me my place. He said that they weren't expecting me for another couple of weeks. He said he was pleased to see me but he didn't look pleased.

My painting has gone from the back wall and the posters that our group made before I got hurt have been taken down.

I don't understand why everyone is staring at me but Natalie was friendly when I hung up my bag.

The twins are staring too. I poke out my tongue at them and turn away.

Suddenly, they are standing beside me. "What happened to your neck?"

The whole room has gone quiet.

I stare ahead at the board, my face burning. "I got burnt."
"How?"

I don't want to say. I don't want to tell them what happened because the words can't show it well enough. The words are not hot enough so that these rude boys can feel how much it hurt. But, I have manners and I am polite so I tell them, tell them all.

There is silence. Then Karen says, "You were lucky, man."

My sister comes to my rescue. "It's because Mum knew what to do, eh Ruth?"

I nod, not wanting to carry on. That's ok because Elizabeth will do it.

"Our mother took off all her clothes and put her straight in a bath of cold water. The doctors told her that was the best thing she did although perhaps she shouldn't have pulled off her clothes."

I print the date in my exercise book. I want her to stop now but I can't look at her because if I do I might cry. Instead, I get up, put my chair in and go to the cloakroom. I hear Elizabeth say as I leave, "But she might get these terrible scars because this guy who worked for us, he grabbed Ruth by the scruff of the neck and has ripped off the new skin."

"Eww, that is so gross."

Someone else says, "Did she get the Crunchie bar?" There is laughter but I don't think it's funny and it feels like they are laughing at me.

Mrs Ward has come out of her room. "Ruth honey, you ok?"

It is then I realise I am crying. I shake my head. "I want to go home," I sniff and she pulls me into her soft tummy. She smells of lavender water and that's not awful, it's just I really do want to go home.

Dad has come to get me. I am relieved. As I get into the truck I say "You still owe me a Crunchie bar." He laughs. He laughs and laughs and although I feel sad, I can feel my face smiling.

"Oh, Ruthie," he says. "You've got a memory like an elephant." He laughs again. "Yes. I do owe you a Crunchie bar. We'll get one on the way back from town."

I wipe my nose and eyes and settle back into the seat. Right now, there's no other place I want to be.

Mum has decided that I'm not ready for school but I try to tell her that it's just that the kids were being mean. She rang Mr Fisher and I think they had an argument because I could hear her getting louder and louder. When she got off the phone, her eyes were bright and her face red like when she shouts at us kids.

But I think she's right because I don't feel safe there. It's like everything is exactly how it was – the smell, the noise, the colours – yet it is too, too different to what I'm used to. I would rather stay home and play with the kitten or go with Dad around the farm or even sit with Mum as she sorts through the piles of washing.

Elizabeth has brought home a whole lot of books for me to read which is good and a special project from Mr Fisher. He has told me I have to find out all about a lady called Helen Keller who was blind and deaf and couldn't speak and how she learned to speak and teach.

For a day I don't speak but no one notices, so the next day, I tie one of Dad's large socks around my head so I can't see and try to do normal things like eat my breakfast and feed the cat and make my bed. Mum says that I've done as good a job as I usually do which is great.

When we go to visit some friends of Dad's in town on the weekend, I get Elizabeth to pretend with me that I can't hear and we giggle because the children shout at me.

The first word Helen Keller learned was water. It was cold and she was angry with her teacher and, as the water from the pump washed over her hands, her kind, patient tutor spelt out the letters W.A.T.E.R over and over until Helen got it finally that the shapes that were being made in her palm were connected to the feel of the water over her hand. That was her moment.

I have turned on the hose outside to make the same shapes with my fingers on my palm as the chilled water flowed but I feel a bit frightened because water means something different to me than it did to Helen Keller: water can be bad, dangerous, it can hurt and hurt and hurt. And, just as happened to her, it can change things forever.

Chapter Twenty

Wards Revisited

Nothing has changed and yet it now seems so weird to me. The sounds, the smells, even the way the sun pours in through the large windows are the same, but the people in the rooms are different, and as yet I do not know any of the nurses. We go up the lifts to my ward and, as the doors sigh open, I can feel myself pulled into the long corridor.

Mum and Dad walk in front. I am looking in each room as we pass thinking that perhaps someone I know might still be there. The sluice room is in the same place; the nurses' office is still there. Dad has gone in but the room is empty.

"Ruth!" a familiar voice calls. I turn to see Matron bustling up from the recreation room. "You look wonderful," she coos but I don't want to look at her. She's not nice and I don't believe this smile she has on her face. "Are you back for a check up?" She asks, pulling linen off one of the trolleys in the corridor.

"No actually, we've come to see a Dr…" Dad pauses while he checks his letter. "Dr Murley."

A flicker of annoyance darts across Matron's face and I feel relieved that the real lady, as I remember her, is still there. However, she still speaks nicely to Dad. "He's on ward rounds; he can't be interrupted I'm afraid."

Dad is about to launch into an argument with her but out of one of the rooms comes a gaggle of white bodies. In the middle is a man whom I recognise from my first time in hospital.

"That's Dr Murley," I say to Dad, pointing.

The doctor hears his name and comes over to us leaving a busy trail of people in white coats. He smiles at us as he shakes Dad's hand and winks at me. For a moment, there is a piece of sunshine in my heart.

The noise has called forth patients from their rooms and I turn to stare at them. Behind us, three girls stand at their open doorway: one has a stuffed wad of gauze over her right eye, tucked under her glasses; the other is on crutches; the last one has a bright red face, shiny and tight. She has been burned. Like me. I don't want to look at her even though she is staring at me.

Suddenly she pokes out her tongue and disappears into the room behind a curtain.

Dad, Mum, and the doctor have moved down the ward to a room I've never seen before. "Ruth!" Mum calls. "Keep up."

I hurry down to them, feeling funny in myself about that girl I've seen.

This morning I had cried because I didn't want to come back. "Please, Mum," I had said. "I don't like that place." Because, the last time I was in hospital, to get my first grafts, I got my period and made the nurse cross because I got blood on the sheet and she carried it on the top of the trolley so everyone could see.

The last time, they forgot to give me painkillers on time and then grumbled because of the noise I made. The last time was the same as the first time because Mum didn't stay and I was afraid.

Christmas Lunch

I've had too much to drink. It's what helps me cope with these gatherings. If I move my head too quickly, though, the room blurs so I stay very still trying to understand the conversation between my mother and the Chinese couple she has brought to Christmas dinner.

Ha. Always caring for waifs and strays, I think meanly.

My sister shoos children outside and arranges the food. She is smiling and puts her arm around Mum's shoulders and chats to the couple before going back to the kitchen. I hate the way she enjoys our mother's company.

My brother Mark's little one climbs onto my lap and plays with my pendant, his fingers sticky with a piece of sucked garlic bread and the contents of his mouth. I don't really like other people's children but I don't want them to know it, so I fuss and pet just as I know I should. He giggles and draws another child, his brother, closer.

"Hello, Sam," I say. "Do you like your new school?" Sam doesn't know me and I don't know him but we are connected to his father so I must be nice.

"Auntie Ruth, what's that on your neck?" he asks pointing to the place where his baby brother is pulling my skin.

My mother answers. "That's where she got burnt, Sam. That's what could happen to you if you're not careful around hot water." Her stock phrase. Me, the excellent example of what will happen to bad children who don't listen to their parents. *Just remember what happened to Ruth,* I have heard her say forever.

"Does it hurt?" Sam is not taking much notice of his Nan. *Right-on, boyo.*

"Not any more. But it did. Once," I say, untangling the baby's grasp from my throat and putting him on the floor. That movement makes my head spin and I sit back carefully.

"What happened?" a younger cousin says, coming in from collecting shells; feeling brave, I suppose, to ask about it in front of this crowd. I think she also knows I'm a bit past it.

I don't want to say, don't want to tell them about how it really was because I feel that if I say it, it will bring up more things I can't see clearly enough yet. Still, I do say "I ran into your grandad who was carrying a pot of hot water. It went all over me."

"Ahh," say the Chinese couple together. "Ahh, very bad thing."

"Yes," I agree. "Terrible."

"Did you cry?" This is Sam.

"No," says Mum. "She was a very brave little girl. She didn't cry at all."

"Yes she did." My sister takes over. "She screamed her lungs out."

Mum and I look at each other.

"I don't remember that," says Mum.

"Me neither," I say. Thinking. "Anyway, I went to hospital for about a month."

The children are impressed. "Wow."

"What's it like in hospital?"

"Ok, I guess," knowing I should say the right things but wanting my mother to hear the truth. "Boring. Nothing to do.

No one comes to see you." I say it out loud for the first time ever. "Your dad came to see me twice," I say to Sam. "And, Grandad once. And Nan twice – the second time to bring me home." It's the booze but it feels good to say it out loud.

"What rubbish," says my sister, taking the covers off the food. "Mum was always at the bloody hospital. I can still smell that cream – what was it called?" She turns to Mum.

"Hydrocortisone," Mum answers her but she is looking at me, funny-like. "I have a jar in the cupboard. Every time I put it on my eczema, I think of Ruthie in hospital."

I can't breathe properly and I try to get the words out. My head is buzzing with a strange thickness. Eventually I spit it out. "What did you say?"

Everyone goes silent. I turn on my sister. "You're wrong," I say. "I should know: I was the one waiting there all the time." I want to yell at them because they don't understand; they never did understand what it was like.

"And I was the one making the trips back in the early hours of the morning," my mother says as she stacks the plates from around the room.

"Mum, I remember!" This time I can hear myself squawking. "I used to lie in bed for hours and hours while every other bloody kid in the ward had their family coming in and out and no one came to see me." The tears are there, pricking at me behind my eyes but I will not let them come.

"You're exaggerating," she says, her mouth a tight line. "As usual."

The Chinese couple have almost shrunk into their seats at the loud conversation. My sister must sense this too because she speaks into the silence. "Anyway, we'd get out of bed in the morning and there wasn't any breakfast like usual. Remember,

Mark? That's how come I'm so good at porridge." She gives me the look. "I took over from Mum."

"Thank goodness." This is Mark's response. "Mum's cooking was awful. Remember the puha?"

"Now, you guys," Mum is saying. "Don't start that again…"

I am not listening. Instead, I am trawling through my memories trying to fish out the image of my mother with me in the hospital. The net keeps coming back empty.

She was not there; I know she was not there. I drink some more of my wine. *I can't see her; I can't remember her and I know I am right.*

I want to cry. I should but I will have to wait until everyone is gone. I need to weep because I am still sad that as a little girl, I did not have my mother when I needed her.

Instead, I go out into the garden to sit with the children. This adult laughter is sand against my wounds.

Mother versus Daughter

I have been summoned home. It doesn't happen often but I could tell by the tone of my mother's voice that it is not something I can avoid.

I ring my sister for advice. "I hate this," I moan. "Why is it always me that ends up with this thing with Mum?"

"I don't know, Ruth. Maybe it's because you're so rude to her."

"I am not rude to her," I protest.

"Crap. You are such a bitch to her. Look at how you behaved at Christmas."

"I was drunk," I say, knowing I had still been aware of what came out of my mouth. Not that I would admit this to her. There is silence on the other end. "You still there?"

"Yeah. You're not always right, you know?"

"Where did that come from?" I am beginning to wish I hadn't called her.

"Well, look at the stuff about Mum visiting you in hospital."

"You know I've got the best memory out of everyone," I say, feeling like I am on the defensive again.

"Not this time. This time we all remember better." She is quiet again but I wait. "You've really upset her you know?"

God, Mum's got to her first, I realise. "Whose side are you on?"

"I'm on no one's side but you need to talk to her."

"Fine," I say, feeling tears. "Fine. I'll go see her."

At home, while Mum gets the tea things, I look at our family photos.

The one in the middle is of Dad, smiling, taken last year. Mark stands behind him with a hand on his shoulder and baby Sam sits on Dad's lap. There's the old photo of us kids bareback on our horses, the colour gone funny but I can see me with my hair long, my head turned away slightly.

I was 12. That summer I took my horse and went camping for the night without telling Mum and Dad. They found me at two in the morning and Mum and I yelled at each other.

There is another of me and my sister during our high school's jubilee. I am frowning at the camera. Just after that photo was taken, Mum and I had a row about me going to the parade. I didn't go. Instead I went down to the park and smoked a packet of her cigarettes. I swallow at the memory: I felt sick as a dog after that.

And this reminds me of the biggest fight of all: both of us yelling because I wanted to go to a party and she wouldn't let me and I called her an uptight bitch and she slapped me and then I slapped her.

I went to the party but we didn't speak for a long time until she asked me to move out.

There are no more of me at that time but lots of the others.

My mother gets straight to the point. "Ruth," she begins. "I'm sorry you think that your dad and I abandoned you while you were in hospital."

"Dad didn't," I say, feeling defensive again. "He came lots of times."

Mum shakes her head. "No he didn't, love. He came twice."

I am pulling at the tufts on the candlewick cushion cover, making holes appear where the strands were attached. She continues. "I was there a lot of the time."

I hate the way she stares at me, just looks at me. It makes me feel funny, like I want to laugh; it is a bit weird. Instead, I press my fingernail into the side of my thumb so that it hurts and I won't smile. She continues. "For the first week, you were in intensive care – remember?" I remember. "Well, you were very sick and they gave you lots of medicine to stop you hurting too much."

This too – not the medicine but the hurt yet I don't tell her this.

Surprisingly I feel tears burn the back of my eyes. "Yes, but I remember …" I begin.

"How can you remember?" She interrupts. "You were ten years old. Ten years old, with third degree burns."

"I have a good memory," I say, lifting my chin defensively.

Mum snorts. "Listen, Ruth, I know what happened; others remember what happened. Don't you think the fact that the rest of the family has the same memories might mean we're right and you're not?"

I look at her, trying to take myself back to that time but it's too difficult. "That's a very good question," I say, my face getting warm. "Still doesn't mean I'm wrong."

"Ruth," Mum begins. "You were very sick. You were barely conscious…"

"Yes, I was," I cry. "I remember them coming and pulling off my skin; I remember that room, that bloody room with the double doors and everyone wearing masks."

"So do I," she says quietly.

I look at her, frowning. "Not like I do!"

"Maybe not, but I was there almost all that time, in that room. It was when they took you into the other one that they said I wasn't allowed to stay."

"You stayed?" This can't be, because I was alone. I was alone in that room with its two-doors and two-doors and the peeling paint.

"It wasn't like it is now. They didn't like people coming in all the time. The doctors told us that you needed to rest as much as possible."

"What about later? When I was sick?" Trying to trick her.

"They wouldn't let any of us in. They told us that there was an infection on the ward."

"They were liars!"

She looks at me, that familiar tired look. "I know that now," she says quietly. "But I didn't know that then. And we were busy on the farm what with the kids getting the chicken pox and Dad getting the new stock…"

I fold my arms and look away. I think of the stories they told us kids: the eel that ate Dad's sock, the bodies in the morgue, the children in the wool press, Santa Claus crashing his helicopter, the taniwha under the bridge.

I think of Dad's hands and his neck where the water burned him. I think of how I thought he was angry at me because I had stopped him from playing his game of tennis and that was why he hadn't been to see me. But I was wrong, he told me so. He'd been hurt and he wasn't angry. Not at all. All those things were not as I had first thought.

And now Mum's telling me she *was* there.

"But, why can't I remember?" I ask again, frustration beginning to choke me.

"Can't you let it go, love?

"No," I cry. "Something's missing for me. Can't you see that?" I stand now, the pain in my chest has moved to my stomach. "There are all these … these … floating pictures; missing parts. I need you to tell me everything. Everything!"

Mum's neck reddens. "I don't know what you want me to say. Even I can't remember everything!" the tone of her voice has changed and I know we have begun to enter one of our fights.

"I want you to tell me why, whenever I needed you, you disappeared on me."

She frowns. "What are you talking about now?"

I throw my hands out. "The hospital, boarding school, hospital again, anything and everything it seems, that was about me, you took a leave of absence."

"That is not true!" she snaps. "The world doesn't revolve around you, Ruth."

"I know that, Mum. And I also know that your not visiting me in hospital is real."

"For goodness' sake, girl. Let it go." She has reached out for me.

"No, Mum." I pull back. I wish I could stop what I am going to say, but I can't, and in a rush, it is out. "When the others talk about how wonderful you are, it makes me feel sick. When they go on about how lovely you are or how much they love you, I feel nothing. I feel nothing for you because I know that's what you feel for me." I feel the words and ideas rushing up and out and I don't want to block any of it. "It's not my fault I have these scars, you know. I didn't mean to run into Dad and I didn't mean for that guy to twist my top. I'm so sorry I'm not as pretty as Elizabeth or as perfect as the boys." The tears are in

130

my mouth, salty, bitter, like the feeling in my gut.

Mum's eyes are wide and there are tears there too but I don't care. I want her to hold some of this pain. "I know you prefer it when I'm not here. That's why you made me stay at the boarding school; why you were so keen for me to go down to Massey."

"Ruth," she cries. "Ruth. This is all wrong. It isn't like that at all."

"Isn't it, Mum? Well you try to tell me how else I am supposed to understand all this." My hands shake and I feel sick. "You tell me what I should have believed."

Round Two

My mother sits forward on the settee. Her lips have gone that pale tight shape they go when she disapproves, usually of me or something I've done. "The reason," she begins, voice clipped, cut, "I wasn't there for your every *friggin'* waking moment, Ruth, was because I was losing a baby!"

It is a slap to my mouth. "What?" I say, somewhat redundantly. "What baby?"

"The baby your father and I made a couple of months before you got burnt." She spits the word 'burnt' at me and it hisses around my ears.

"A miscarriage?" I'm trying to rearrange the picture of my childhood to accept this new information. A baby? Mum had been pregnant then? I can't quite take it in. "Why didn't you say, Mum?" My anger has been blunted momentarily.

Then I'm thinking, she could have saved herself some angst if she'd told me. I breathe deeply and level this at her: "You could have said, all those years ago, and then I wouldn't have thought badly of you."

"What right do you have to feel bad about me anyway?" she asks, the stern voice of old returning. Her eyes drill me and I'm ten again; we are back to being mother and child, not two adults. "You had everything we could give you – all of you did." She points to me, her finger shaking, daring me to answer back like

I've done many times before. Daring me to argue to the point where I'm sent to my room.

And me, I'm trying not to be that ten-year-old again; I am trying to think on my feet, to come up with an answer to this – one that makes sense for both of us. One that is adult, conciliatory. "I felt angry because I needed you and you weren't there." This isn't working; I can tell from her eyes but I stumble on. "I didn't know why; no one told me why and if they had, it would have been ok with me, Mum. But all I remember is that you weren't there. Your memories are different because you have always had the whole picture. And, I've grown up so angry with you for leaving me." I am now completely exposed, in the nuddy, and I feel as raw as I did when my skin was new.

She applies the sandpaper. "You're wrong: I didn't leave you. I *was* there." Her voice rises again.

She still doesn't get it. It's not about the facts; it's about what I remember and what I was feeling and how that makes me feel now. But, I'm not giving up. "Not all the time. Not when I was asking for you. Not for when it mattered to me you weren't, and no one told me why." My voice rises to match hers.

"For God's sake Ruth – get over it! It's in the past. It's done with and I can't take it back – I can't take back that you got burnt; I can't take back that I lost a baby; I can't take any of it back." I have not seen her so worked up for a long while. "Stop punishing me for not being perfect." Her voice breaks and she is breathing heavily. "I did the best I could, girl. I tried my best and that's what you got from me."

We are standing, facing each other. The air is thick with humidity and our passion. I can feel sweat running between my shoulder blades and prickling my top lip.

I swallow the thickness in my throat. "Can you not tell me,

not as a little girl but as an adult? Can you not let me in even just a little bit? For both of us?"

She looks at me for a while but she's not seeing me, I can tell. Eventually, she sighs deeply before speaking. "It was an accident – the pregnancy. Your father and I didn't want any more kids – four was enough. So, when you got hurt, *and* your dad, and then the chicken pox with the kids, it was to be expected…"

The pit of my stomach chills as I realise what she's saying. "Was it my fault?" I ask, tears there again.

Mum looks up from her hands. "It wasn't your *fault* Ruth. It just wasn't meant to be. That's the way we saw it then and the way I see it now."

"Pity," I say.

"I don't see it like that. And, you're not to tell your sister."

"Mum, you have to. She has to know the truth," I cry.

"Really, Ruth? Do you really think so? What truth do you want her to know? She's already got her history sorted – it's you who's going around stirring up the water looking for mud crabs. *Just let it go.*"

But I can't. I think I need her to say it out loud to me again. "I need you to tell me the whole lot."

"Why?" She cries, her tone intensifying.

"Because it's important to me. So that maybe I can go forward and … I don't know … pack it away neatly for once and for all."

"You always were a persistent little bugger." She pulls the stray strands of greying hair into the tie at the back of her head. "Let's go down to the beach. It's too bloody hot in here."

So, as we walk, I piece together her story with mine. And, at the same time, fill in the background of our shared history:

That year, that time I lay in a hospital bed having skin scraped from me, she was in hospital too, she was losing a baby. *That's why she couldn't come* I whisper in my heart to the burnt little girl who was me, *you were right, there was something wrong but it wasn't your fault*: because I knew even then that things were not right. I remember because of the way Dad had reacted, and the nurses, and how Mum had looked that time she did visit – so skinny and tired looking.

She tells me other things: "Those horrible gowns and the masks and on the first night you trying to escape." She lets out a small laugh. "You were so determined. I asked you where you thought you were going. "I am going to go home," you'd said. The nurse told me you were delirious. Mostly that first week you slept."

I am surprised at how much relief there is to have someone else say out loud the details of what has been hidden in my memory for so long. "Do you remember when they dressed me?" I am that little girl again, but walking beside her, safe in the sunlight.

"I hated looking so I used to just sit by the window. Sometimes I held your hand. It was easier for them when you were asleep.

"For the first week, you were in intensive care and were pretty much out to it. Then they shifted you out into the two-bed room with the girl with the burnt face –"

"Kiri."

"Kiri. You weren't really well enough to leave ICU but another burns child had come in and they needed the bed."

"I don't think I ever saw him," I say.

"He died about two weeks later."

"Oh. Poor parents."

"It was pretty terrible all right. He was only four. I even re-member his name: Stephen Alexander. He pulled a pot over himself and his dad threw him into the cow's trough because it was the closest water but he got an infection and they couldn't save him. They tried everything. I overheard one of the nurses say they tried some new type of medication but even that didn't work."

I cast my mind back to the ward and try to conjure up an awareness of that story. It doesn't really work and I feel cheated that I didn't know about him.

Then, she tells me other things, later things that are still connected to that time:

The year I discovered boys, was rebelling and sneaking out of the dorm to meet them down by the pools, was the year my mother spent two weeks in hospital, having a hysterectomy. In the town where I was miserable. And, I never knew. I could have visited her.

I look over at her and wonder what else she has stored in her own memories; what other stories are playing out that I don't know of. I get this overwhelming urge to learn everything about her, and how things were and are for her. It is a strange feeling because it is new and it is like seeing someone properly, up close, for the first time, not hidden behind familiar smells and memories and attachments. This woman who walks beside me is someone like me.

This realisation floods my chest and stops me right there.

"Mum," I cry. She must hear something in my voice because she spins around and pulls me into a hug. "I'm sorry," I say, choking the words out.

"It's all right, Ruthie," she murmurs, letting me sob into her neck. She goes to step back but I'm not finished with her yet and grab her tighter. "You silly chicken," she chuckles, rubbing my back.

As I hold her, I am reclaiming the missed bits of her but she's had enough. "Ruth, people are staring."

I break away, eyes still wet, and try to grin at the old couple who are frowning at us. God knows what they think is going on. Then I link my arm through Mum's and we continue along the sand, both of us wiping our eyes and sniffing at the same time. We look at each other and laugh out loud. Yes, that couple must think we're completely bonkers but I don't care because I've just gained something I thought I'd lost nearly ten years ago.

Records

"Plowman," I say to the young woman at the doctor's surgery. She nods and goes out the back as I lean against the counter feeling stupid.

And excited.

The door bangs open again very soon and she is holding a pile of yellowed files. "There are two records for 'R. Plowman'. Your mum's and yours." I wonder at the story my mother's folder holds but shake away the curious thoughts. The receptionist hands me a folder. "This is your one. Check through them and anything you want copied, make a note and I'll do it."

"Cheers," I say. "I'll be back soon."

I go into one of the small rooms reserved for locums and sit at the small desk.

I am the only one here apart from the staff; not surprising – it is summer, the holidays, and every good family is at the beach, or by a river, or staying on a farm, or anywhere but working or hunting for secrets and chasing memories.

The file is marked and tattered but the yellowed white label is achingly familiar – the same numbers and letters, the same information, the same print type that was on my bracelet which ensnared my wrist for a month:

PLOWMAN, R   F

d.o.b 1st Sept 1962

NHN: DHH6778556

Inside, forms, attached and loose, are clipped together with the old spear-type paper clips. I press the spine of the folder and pick up my pen. The one on top is my discharge form. I shuffle through the papers until I get to the first sheet. The beginning.

The ink is faded and the handwriting messy, but I am used to Anton's illegible handwriting so I can understand the swirls and lines. And now I can read the story of this patchy memory:

Ruth Plowman
female, 10 yrs, 5 mths
burns, hot water, face, chest, left arm and left knee, upper back
post 60mins
ran into father. placed in cold bath. clothes removed before bath.
3rd º neck (r. side), r. chin, r. ck
2nd º face, l. arm and l. knee, back
approx 32%
IV 5120cc/8/24
BP 100/70
P 160
Temp 36

There is an A4 envelope at the back of my folder; the type that holds X-rays. A large stamp of numbers sits proudly at the top -- some are the same as those on the front label but there are some extra which make no sense to me.

Inside these are three bits of paper: one, like a time sheet which is half filled in with numbers and times and dates and notes; another is a carbon copy of a typed letter, at the bottom of which is my mother's signature, hastily scrawled next to the date of my accident. The last page is a faded form with a letterhead from Kelton Pharmaceuticals. This I read first:

Dariomyson Trial # 4
Patient No: DHH6778556
Start date: 13/02/73
End date: 05/03/73
Batch: 03/1973
I go back and read the form signed by my mother:

Permission for Medical Treatment
I hereby authorise the hospital representative to secure whatever medical treatment is deemed necessary such as immunisation or other inoculation programmes as determined by hospital authorities.

Signed Mrs Rosemary Plowman

I make a note to copy these three and then turn back to my notes from the ward: here is an account of how long I was in ICU (one week), HDU (three days), the ward (the rest of the time). There is a note about us leaving the ward without permission (when we found the morgue) and when I got sick. There is also a strange sentence on its own:
began trial a.m.

The reason it is strange is that the word 'experiment' has been crossed out and 'trial' written above by another hand.

More News

I have found someone who remembers, the note says. *Ring me when you can. Steve.* The note is dated before Christmas, weeks ago, time enough for me to grab a hold of my memories and make more sense of them.

Nevertheless, I dial the newspaper and apologise for missing his message.

"Your experiment story. It's really just died a natural death, I'm sorry to say. I did some checking and found someone who was involved. It's one of the nurses," Steve tells me. "She told me quite a lot."

I can feel butterflies in my stomach. "What did she say?"

"She said that the hospital received special funding to administer the drug: that it was rushed through because there was some urgency. That it was part of the whole immunisation programme."

"But it wasn't immunisation."

"I know. That's what I said. Apparently, parents did give permission for inoculation – they just didn't know what else they were giving permission for."

"Yeah, that's what I found in my notes too. Something my mum signed. Good grief. That gave them the right to do anything."

"Exactly. So, that's why there's really no story."

"You're wrong you know," I say, letting my frustration come to the surface. "There is a story – mine. And I'm bloody pissed off that they were allowed to do that to us, get away with it and there's nothing we can do." I feel armed and ready, now that the aching holes of my mother's absences are accounted for. Ready to turn my anger onto these nameless, faceless people who used me. "You know what?" I tell him. "I feel like we were violated."

"I can understand you must be pretty upset."

I snort. "That's an understatement."

It is a moment before he answers. "I've done as much as I can. Sorry but I'm onto other things now. Best of luck, eh?" I am being dismissed.

"Yeah. Thanks for your help." I say, bitterly and go to hang up, but Steve speaks. "What was that?" I ask.

"I said, the nurse said none of you were in any danger."

"I'm sure," I reply sarcastically. "No danger at all. What with children with illness and injury – "

"No, it wasn't the kids with illness. Just the kids with injuries or needing ops. That's what she said. You weren't on a medical ward – there was another children's ward for sick kids."

I am surprised because I never knew this. I thought we were all there was. But, as I think about it, I realise that he must be right because we all had things wrong on the outside or to do with bones; none of us was sick with a disease.

But then I think of something. "Wait a minute. There *is* more. My mother told me the other day about this kid in the hospital who had burns too. He died."

"That happens."

"Steve, quit the sarcasm eh? But, he may not have had to die. They used the drug on him."

"How do you know?"

"Mum said she heard the nurses say that they had tried every-thing, even this new drug. And, it was two *weeks* after he was admitted that he died."

"That would make it about the same time as …"

"As we all got the bugs," I interrupt. "That's right. Your nurse was wrong. He would have been too sick to have the bugs and maybe they panicked and gave him the medicine and it didn't work and then they covered it up." I'm getting excited now. There could be a story.

"Wait, wait, wait. I'll have to do some finding out. Can you give me a name?"

"Yes. Um. No. I can't remember it, but my mum knows it." I remember Mum asking me not to talk to her about that time again. Perhaps just one more question would be all right. "I think I can get it."

"I hope so," he says and then the phone clicks off.

Then, there is another message. This time from my sister.

"You're not going to believe this," she laughs. "There's this girl at my gym, Ruth. She's got her little boy to have these tests on his hips. And she told us all about how she and her brother had to spend weeks in hospital in casts up to their armpits."

"What's her name?" I ask, excited, nervous.

"Aleea."

"That's one of them," I almost squeal. "She and her brother Tom. They were there too."

I feel like I do when I'm at a party, meeting people for the first time and we trace back our histories trying to find the common ground, checking out name, rank and serial number:

You went to Girls' High, too? When? Really? Do you remember Mr Taffs – wasn't he a scream?

Or, you find the people connection:

Plowman, eh? I remember some Plowmans who lived next door to my granddad's place up north. That's your family? Oh my God! What a small world!

This connectedness seems surreal – my two separate lives have become a little attached.

Elizabeth continues. "Well, she got married to the son of the chemist – Lance Reynolds. God, do you remember how we thought he was such a hunk?"

I laugh but I am remembering. Remembering the soft, wet mouth, thin lips, the red-dark room of the garage where we had gathered for Shona's party. I remember not liking him and not liking his kissing. Worried he would see my scars; feel them so I wouldn't let him touch me and then he had told everyone I was frigid.

Witness

There is nothing about her that I recognise. She is tall and thin, her hair cropped bluntly just above the shoulders.

She stayed in the area. Just like Elizabeth. And Elizabeth knows everyone.

"How old are the kids?" I ask, being polite.

"Ruby's three and Daniel's one and a half."

I figure it's no use trying small talk with her as I can sense she is not happy about my interruption into her daily routine. "Aleea, how much do you remember about being in hospital for your hips?"

"Everything. Don't you?"

I nod. "Pretty much most things. But, we all remember different things don't we?"

She shrugs but puts the little boy down. He stands beside her, clinging to her leg. "What I'm here for, Aleea, is to see how much you know about the test they did on us."

She looks to her wrist and then I know she knows; she remembers, and it proves that I'm not crazy. "What about it?"

'Didn't you ever wonder what it was about?"

"They told us. It was just a test to see how healthy we were. Wasn't it like some sort of medical survey?"

"No. They used us to trial a new drug."

She stares at me. I don't think she believes it. "How do you know that?"

"This reporter, he found out that's what they were doing in the sixties and seventies and so I checked in my records. It's all there. It wasn't a secret."

"So it must have been ok then."

"No. It wasn't ok. You don't just give kids bugs and then try to make them better. We were us; people; not bloody lab rats." My voice is getting louder and I can tell, in this house, no one's voice gets loud. The boy is sucking his thumb now, still clinging to her leg. Aleea is frowning at my tone. I cough, lowering my voice. "I didn't say they could do it on me; I don't think you did either. My mum and dad certainly didn't know what was going on…"

"Listen, Ruth. It was a long time ago. So some of us got a bit sick; no one got hurt. They were doing their job."

I'm frustrated. Aleea is not like me: she's a good citizen; a good mother, grateful, doesn't make a fuss, doesn't like a fuss made; perhaps doesn't like thinking about the past.

"It was wrong." The words come out quietly but I am angry still and she sees it. "This friend, this reporter, he wants to do a story about what happened as part of a larger story. He said it would be good to get more people to talk about the experiment…"

"Sorry, Ruth. I'm not interested in the past. I don't want to be involved in anything like that." She is shaking her head and I can see that I am losing her.

"But, Aleea …"

"No, Ruth. I'm sorry." She has picked up the boy again. "I can't help you."

And I am dismissed. I can serve no purpose for her or her family.

"Ok. Fair enough," I say thinking I can smooth waters;

thinking of another angle. "What about Tom? Perhaps Tom might be interested."

"I doubt it. Tom's in prison. In Auckland." Tight lips; hard eyes.

There is silence. What am I supposed to say to that? "I'm sorry," I say. Truthfully, because I am. I liked her brother. "Well, if you're talking to him, perhaps you could …"

She's the polite hostess now. "I'm sorry I can't help you."

I get up and make my way to her front door. "Thanks for your time, Aleea."

But, just as she closes the door says, "Good luck."

Department of Corrections
Auckland Prison Paremoremo
P O Box Albany

Dear Ruth,

Thanks for your letter. I do remember those tests. I didn't get sick, bear in mind, so I didn't have to have the puke-making medicine. Still happy to help in any way I can, though – I've got some time on my hands (so to speak). Send me what you've got so far. Look forward to hearing from you.

Tom

Ending and Starting

Anton puts Tom's letter on the bench. "So, you've got some more support. What do you want to do now?"

His question surprises me: first because he doesn't know, and second because I don't think I really know either. "I think I want people to go, 'Oooh; that's terrible. We must do something to make sure it doesn't happen again.'"

"But, they don't do that any more, do they?"

"You would hope not. And that's what's so bloody frustrating." I chew my lip, trying to grab at the words and phrases that are leaping around inside me. "I think I want to be able to go back to the ward, back then, and tell them off." I see how stupid it sounds and he laughs with me.

His eyes twinkle. "I can see it really burns you up."

I groan. "That is so lame, Anton. Stick to plants."

He taps the letter. "Why don't you just drop it now? Let this Tom fellow take over?"

I shake my head. "I can't. Now I've started something, I've got to see it through. It's a matter of principle. I can't explain this very well, ok? I just need to finish it."

"Fair enough." He takes my hand in his. "It isn't going to happen quickly."

I nod but I've been hanging onto this for so long I'm used to the weight of it. "I'm in no hurry."

I don't want it all to go to waste: the burns, the time in the ward, the testing on us with the drug, the spewing up and the loneliness of missing my family. I'd hate for all of this emotional energy I've invested, holding on to these memories, just to be shelved – like a book that's read once but never re-read.

"There's got to be something positive in it for me."

"I know," he replies. "Just don't let it take over your life."

"You mean like you and your seedlings?" I toss at him.

"Exactly!" he grins and pulls me around to his side of the bench. "Because I'm hopeful one of us will leave here and get a real job." He kisses the side of my neck and this time I don't move away. This time I smile and move closer, feeling ok about him touching my scars, ok about my mother and ok about where these investigations might take me.

Epilogue: Grafts

The anesthetist has already been in to see me and I didn't ask him for something to take away my nerves. I didn't think I would be this frightened so, as they wheel me down the corridors, I fix my eyes on Anton's anxious face.

He has stopped at the theatre doors and mouths that he loves me. I don't have time to tell him anything because the doctor has been waiting.

"Hop over to this bed," the nurse says, her voice slightly muffled through her mask. My stomach is sore and my throat dry. Nothing will go wrong, I tell myself as they arrange me on the skinny operating table and drape large sheets over my shoulders.

"Comfy?" my surgeon asks but I just want to cry. He pats my shoulder. "Don't worry, Ruth. I'll take great care of you."

"You'll just feel a wee prick," the anesthetist says and the panic increases as I feel the heaviness surge up my arm.

"Ruth," someone is shouting. "All done. We're just going to put this under you, ok?" Not that I can speak. I feel sick and need to wee. "How you feeling?" the shouting again.

"Sick," I mumble.

I think they will bring me a bowl but I get a sting in my

thigh instead. "That'll make you feel better in a moment." The shouting still. Wish she'd stop yelling.

A phone rings. Bloody hell, I think. Can't a girl get some peace and quiet?

Not shouting this time but a chirpy young voice. "Yes, she's out now. Everything's fine. Went really well. She's doing great. Ok. I'll tell her."

When she talks to me, it is different to her phone voice though. "That was your mum, Ruth. She sends her love and will be over to see you soon," the shouting nurse calls.

"I love my mum," I know I say, feeling silly for saying it, tears beginning to dribble down the side of my face.

"Hey, none of that," another nurse fusses. "You'll wet the bandages." She dabs at my face. "Why the tears?"

"Just my mum," I try to say, but it doesn't come out right. "I'm glad she called."

"Course you are. Now, you go to sleep and we'll be right here if you need us," she says sweetly.

She has brought a crossword book and some chocolates.

"How are you?" she asks kissing me on the forehead like I am a child.

I am surprised how pleased I am to see her. "Only hurts if I turn my head too quickly," I reply, reaching out for her hand. She sits on the edge of the bed and looks about the room.

"Who's doing the milking?" I ask, working out what time it is and almost hearing and smelling the ladies lining up along the fence line in front of the cowshed gates.

"Mark's helping Dad. I can't have you accuse me of abandoning you this time," she says, smirking.

I try to smile at her. She's a tough bird, my mum. "I'm glad you came," I say, looking at her, trying to understand her. "You can help me with the tricky words."

Author's Note:

In 1973, I suffered third degree burns in much the same manner as Ruth. While I was in hospital, all the children in the ward were injected with some type of bacteria (the nurses used the same instrument I describe in Chapter Six) and then, if we got sick (as I did), were given a foul-tasting, creamy medicine to 'make us better'. My mother had no knowledge that this 'test' or 'experiment' took place. The hospital has no record of my time there as all records (except maternity patients) pre-1990 have been destroyed.